The Rauermans

Part 2

Albert Sandberg

The Sandberg Series Book 2

TotalRecall Publications, Inc.
1103 Middlecreek
Friendswood, Texas 77546
281-992-3131   281-482-5390 Fax
www.totalrecallpress.com

All rights reserved. Except as permitted under the United States Copyright Act of 1976, No part of this publication may be reproduced, stored in a retrieval system, or transmitted in any form or by any means electronic or mechanical or by photocopying, recording, or otherwise without prior permission of the publisher. Exclusive worldwide content publication / distribution by TotalRecall Publications, Inc.

Copyright © 2020 by: Albert Sandberg
Edited by Sigrid MacDonald, Book Magic
Cover photo by Shutterstock - Nejron Photo
All rights reserved
ISBN: 978-1-59095-557-4
UPC: 6-43977-45579-6

Printed in the United States of America with simultaneous printings in Australia, Canada, and United Kingdom.

FIRST EDITION
1 2 3 4 5 6 7 8 9 10

This book is a work of fiction. It reflects the author's knowledge of the lives of his ancestors. All other characters, names, events, views, and subject matter of this book are either the author's imagination or are used fictitiously. Any similarity or resemblance to any real people, real situations or actual events is purely coincidental and not intended to portray any person, place, or event in a false, disparaging or negative light.

The scanning, uploading and distribution of this book via the Internet or via any other means without the permission of the publisher is illegal and punishable by law. Please purchase only authorized electronic editions, and do not participate in or encourage electronic piracy of copyrighted materials. Your support of the author's rights is appreciated.

To the memories of my grandparents,
Donald and Catherine Bradburn

Chapter 1
Sörfors, Sweden
August 1777

"Push now, Sig!"
"I can't!"
"Push! Now!"

Sigrid Jonsdotter was having trouble delivering her eleventh child. Her friend and midwife, Lovisa Öhn, was urging her through the difficulty. Dárjá, Lovisa's stepdaughter, was assisting her. With a scream, Sigrid pushed hard, and little Jakob slid out, followed by a large flow of blood.

"Oh!" Dárjá gasped.

"What?" Sigrid cried; she was alarmingly pale and covered with sweat.

"I'm sorry, Sig. He's dead," Lovisa said, handing the baby to Dárjá.

"Nej!" Sigrid cried, "Not another one!" Sigrid, and her husband, Emanuel Raderman, had lost four other children between the ages of one and seven. They were in Emanuel and Sigrid's cabin, in their bedroom. Emanuel and their children, Olaus thirteen, Maria eight, Jonas seven, Emanuel Junior six, Margareta five and Barbro three, sat quietly at the kitchen table listening to the muffled gasps and cries coming from the bedroom. They were no strangers to loss and heartache, but there was still a sense of dread this time as they looked down at the table.

"Manni!" Lovisa called. "Bring some more cloth and water!"

Emanuel jumped and then hustled his children outside. "Stay outside until I call you," he said and then went to get the cloth. He tapped on the door and then entered the bedroom. Emanuel had witnessed field amputations and battlefield gore during the Pomeranian War, but he was not prepared for what he now saw.

"Here!" Lovisa cried, "Bring them here!"

Emanuel started and then hurried to his wife, handing the cloths to Lovisa, Dárjá taking the pail of water from him.

"Is she…?"

"Nej, she's sleeping," Lovisa answered quietly. She looked Emanuel in the eye. "You should stay with her, say your goodbyes if she wakes up." Tears were running down Lovisa's cheeks; she did not try to hide them. Sigrid did not wake up. She died the next day. It would be the last time Lovisa performed the duties of a midwife.

Chapter 2
Hössjö
The Tiäder Farm

Tobias Öhn became Soldier Öhn on his nineteenth birthday. The army did not see any reason to assign him a new soldier's name as Öhn was a unique name in its own right. Upon entering military service, new recruits were often assigned a new surname. The practice was necessary due to the Swedish patronymic naming system where the child's surname would consist of his or her father's first name, followed by son or dotter. So, for instance, all of Olof's sons would have the surname Olofsson, and all his daughter's surnames would be Olofsdotter. This did not work so well in the military as there would be many Larssons, Jonssons, Erikssons and so on. The new surname may be based on where the recruit was from, his physical attributes or his trade. Names such as Berg (mountain), Stark (strong), Svärd (sword), Björn (bear) or Lång (tall) were common.

Tobias was assigned the Tiäder croft near Hössjö. His mother and stepfather had argued against his joining the Swedish army, but for different reasons. His mother, Lovisa, lost her fiancé, and Tobias's natural father, Pehr Raderman, to the Pomeranian War. She did not want Tobias to go through a similar experience, should another war take place. His stepfather, Dánel, opposed his joining for the simple reason that Dánel was Sámi, and held no allegiance to Sweden. His was part of a group of nomadic people, spending equal amounts of time in Norway and Sweden and occasionally Finland.

Tobias was feeding his chickens when Lovisa and Dárjá rode into his farmyard.

"Välkommen, Mamma, sister!" Tobias called.

"Hej, Toby!" Dárjá cried, leaping off her horse and running to him. Tobias scooped her up and spun her around, eliciting shrieks of joy from his sister. Dárjá was five years older than Tobias, accepting him as her brother the moment they met. They were inseparable in their childhood, Dárjá always watching out for him.

"Mamma," he said, putting Dárjá down and embracing his mother, "is something wrong?"

"Siggy died; her baby too."

"I am sorry, Mamma. I know how much she meant to you."

"I want to go lie down for a while, Toby," Lovisa said. She was clearly exhausted — physically and emotionally drained.

"Of course, Mamma," Tobias said. "Dárjá and I will go for a walk to the creek to see if we can catch us a fish for dinner."

Shortly after being assigned to the rote, Tobias discovered a prime fishing spot on the bank of a creek about a half-mile from his croft. He found it relaxing to go there in the evening after dinner. More often than not, he would release the fish he caught, quite content with the excitement and satisfaction the act of catching and landing a fish provided. Over the summer, Tobias had cleared an area where the trail emerged at the creek. He had then cut back some of the cattails and reeds so his fishing hooks would not snag on them. He had also built a chair using diamond willow and lashed with smaller willows stripped of bark. Tobias was of the opinion that it may have been the most comfortable chair he ever sat in, as long as he remembered to bring a fur for padding. Today, he would give Dárjá the honor of catching a fish, but not the honor of sitting in his chair. He baited the hook and passed the rod to her.

"Just fling it sidearm as far as you can."

"I have done this before, Toby!"

Tobias sat in his chair while Dárjá remained standing.

"You know, it is customary, among civilized folks, that is, to offer your guest a chair!"

"Ja?" Tobias said, "I wouldn't know, being raised a savage by my older sister."

"Hah!" Dárjá snorted, then more seriously, "Pappa has been acting strangely since you left."

"How so?" Tobias asked.

"It's hard to explain," Dárjá said. "He forgets where he puts things and then accuses others of stealing."

"Really?"

"Ja, and he loses his temper at the slightest thing," Dárjá continued. "I was glad when Mamma asked me to come with her to help Sigrid."

"Has he hurt you, or Mamma?" Tobias asked, alarmed.

"Nej, but I think it is possible. He is getting worse every day."

"Then you and Mamma will stay here!" Tobias said.

"The people are all I know. I cannot leave them," Dárjá said.

They were silent for a while, each in their own thoughts until a fish nibbled on the hook.

"Let him bite it. Then give it a good jerk," Tobias said.

"I know how to fish, Toby!" Dárjá said as she jerked the rod only to see her hook go flying by her head.

"Ja, I can see that."

"Just bait the hook, Toby!"

"You are such a good fisher. You bait it!"

"Fine!" Dárjá said, "Probably why the fish let go. The hook wasn't baited properly!"

She walked along the shore poking in the reeds until she found and grabbed a small frog. Tying it to her hook, she flung it out and watched the cork bob in the middle of the stream. The cork moved about as the frog tried to swim away, first one way, then another.

"It is good to see you again, brother," Dárjá said when she sat on the ground beside his chair. "How was the general muster?"

The general muster, or GM, was the gathering of an entire regiment every three years for training and inspection. It would last for three weeks and was attended by twelve hundred soldiers from all eight companies that made up the Västerbotten Regiment. Tobias belonged to the Överstelieutnant Company. At the GM, Tobias would participate in exercises, training and shooting practice. The other companies that made up the Västerbotten Regiment were Bygdeå, Kalix, Lövångers, Majorens, Piteå and the LivKompaniet.

"It was tough, but Erik Kiällberg helped me through it."

"Erik?" Dárjá asked, "Manni and Sigrid's son?"

"Ja, well, not really their son." Tobias related what Erik had told him one evening, "Sigrid and her first husband, Johan Berg, took him in when Erik's parents died from the fever. After Johan died in the war, Emanuel took Sigrid for his wife and assumed care of Erik until he became a man."

"Ja, I remember Erik now," Dárjá said. "He and Manni had a sawmill up the Umeå River. We went there a few times when we were small and swam in the river."

"Ja!" exclaimed Tobias. "That's right; I forgot about that!"

Dárjá's rod began twitching. This time she calmly jerked the rod when she felt a good tug on the hook and successfully set it. She began winding the line, letting it out when the fish pulled hard and wound the line when it slackened. She was clearly enjoying the fight and Tobias watched her with both pleasure and pride. When the fish was brought near shore, Dárjá waited for it to put tension on the line before masterfully slinging the rod and landing the fish on the shore.

"That's a nice Gädda [pike], Dárjá!" exclaimed Tobias. "Good work!"

"Ja, now I will give you the honor of cleaning it."

"Nej, sister, you catch, you clean!" Tobias said, grinning. "That is rule number one of the Öhn-Tiäder farm!"

"Ja, okay, brother," Dárjá said, "even though you just made up that rule!"

They walked along the beaten earth path through the bush to the road leading to his farm. The path was a mix of spruce and poplar trees with the odd birch closer to the creek.

"I will ask Mamma to stay for a few days," Tobias said as they stepped onto the dirt road. "Is that okay with you?"

"Ja, I will enjoy the visit," Dárjá said, "and your cabin could use a good cleaning; smells like fart."

"Hah!" laughed Tobias.

"You must have been eating turnips again!"

Tobias inherited his mother's flatulent reaction to turnips, but on a much larger scale.

"I don't particularly enjoy eating turnips, though," observed Tobias.

"Then why do you?"

"Because I enjoy the farts!" Tobias cried, grabbing Dárjá by the head and pulling her down near his rear as he grunted.

Dárjá shrieked and Tobias said, "Ach, skit!"

"What?" Dárjá began, then, "Ugh! Did you just skit your pants?"

"Ja, I tried to fart, but got a turtle head instead!" Tobias said, clearly embarrassed and waddling over to the bush along the road.

"What?" Dárjá called after him, "what's a turtle head?"

"It's when just a little poop pokes out, like a turtle's head poking out of its shell."

Dárjá burst into laughter and called, "I will go clean and cook this fish. Dárjá rule number one; I do not wash poopy pants!"

****

"Where is Toby?" Lovisa asked when Dárjá came into the cabin alone.

"He pooped his pants!"

"What!" Lovisa cried, "Why would he do that; is he ill?"

"He was trying to fart in my face!" Dárjá said, laughing at the memory.

"That boy!" Lovisa said, shaking her head but grinning just the same. "He will never grow up!"

"He wants us to stay for a few days."

"That is good; I would like to go to Siggy's funeral," Lovisa said, her eyes moist. Sigrid had been Lovisa's closest friend for the past twenty years, since the death of Sigrid's first husband, Johan. After Johan died, Sigrid was forced to leave the soldier's croft and Lovisa took her in until she remarried. Sigrid's second husband was the soldier Emanuel Raderman-Apelfeldt, brother of Lovisa's then fiancé, soldier Pehr Raderman-Rask.

Pehr had survived the Pomeranian War, suffering a head wound that caused him to lose his memory. After regaining his memory, the army accused him of desertion and hunted him down, ending with what she believed was his death on the old Viking trail that ran through the Scandinavian mountains. What she didn't know was Pehr had survived and was taken back to Trondheim by his old friend, the Norwegian policeman, Axel Paulsen.

Tobias was the same age as Pehr was when he joined the army. The resemblance was uncanny, a constant reminder to Lovisa, and Pehr's brothers, of Pehr. Lovisa never really got over losing Pehr. Indeed, her marriage to Dánel was one of convenience rather than love. Her love for her stepdaughter, Dárjá, though, was just as deep as her love for her natural son, Tobias.

"Where is he?"

"I think he went back to the creek to wash himself, and his pants," Dárjá said with a grin.

Lovisa looked at her and they both began laughing.

"Let's cook that fish," she said after they recovered, "and don't tease Pehr when he comes in."

"What did you say?"

"I said, don't tease him."

"Nej, you called him Pehr."

"Did I?" Lovisa asked quietly, looking out the window.

"Ja, you did."

"It is nothing; go get a bucket of water for the turnips."

Tobias's croft was small, as soldier crofts go, 12' x 16' with no loft. The walls were tight-fitting squared logs and a pole roof covered with birch bark and sod. The bedroom was 6' x 9', the kitchen/dining room 10' x 12'. The remaining 3' x 6' area was divided into two closets, one in the bedroom and the other off the main room. Two small windows and one door completed the croft. It was, for sure, a bachelor's croft. Much to Dárjá's delight, it was very easy to clean. The farm itself was also quite small, two acres including his yard. A small barn for seed and feed storage, the only livestock, three chickens. Of course, Tobias always had plenty of reindeer meat from the Sámi to last throughout the winter. His summer fare was fresh and salted fish, berries, beans and root vegetables from his small garden. Growing up in a nomadic lifestyle, Tobias was not much of a farmer, so he let his neighbor plant crops on the remaining acre or so. The arrangement worked well for both parties, Tobias receiving bread and pork now and then as payment.

Chapter 3
Vännäsby Church

Olof Raderman steered his wagon into the churchyard, finding a shaded area where he could tie his horse. His wife, Katarina Tobiasdotter, sat beside him and their four daughters, Anna fourteen, Brita twelve, Kajsa ten and Stina nine, sat in the bed of the wagon, all in their church dresses. They leaped out the back of the wagon when it came to a stop and bolted to where other children were playing.

"Be respectful, children!" Olof yelled after them, perhaps a bit too loud as everyone in the church grounds looked their way.

Today was the funerals of his brother's wife and child. Emanuel stood near the church steps with his three-year-old daughter, Barbro, fidgeting beside him. Emanuel accepted condolences from friends and parishioners as they walked past him into the church. His other children, Olaus, Maria, Jonas, Emanuel Junior and Margareta, were sitting on two benches in front of the church. They had endured the sad looks and murmurs of 'oh, those poor children.' Many women tried to embrace them, but they stayed stiffly on the benches, heads down, hands in their laps.

"Hej, Manni," Olof said when they got to Emanuel. "I am sorry. We all loved Sigrid."

"Tack, Olof, Katarina."

"Katarina, can you take Barbro inside and find us seats?" Olof said, "I will stand with Manni for a while."

"Of course, Olof; come, Barbro," she said, taking her hand.

"Tack, Olof," Emanuel said gratefully. Emanuel was no stranger to loss; death was not so rare in this time and place. He has lost three daughters and one son in infancy and now his wife and another son.

"Oh, no! What is she doing here?" Olof said, spotting Lovisa, her daughter and son as they rode into the churchyard aboard impressive mountain horses. "I will tell her she is not welcome here!"

"Nej, Olof, she is welcome here!" Emanuel said forcefully. "She was Sigrid's closest friend; they were like sisters."

"But she was the midwife when…"

"Olof, it was not her fault; she did everything she could!" Emanuel said, cutting him off, "She will always be welcome!"

"Okay, Manni," Olof said. He had, for years, a strained relationship with Lovisa.

Lovisa, Dárjá and Tobias staked their horses in the shade of a large oak tree and began walking toward the church.

Emanuel's children stood when Lovisa came near. She knelt and the children crowded around their auntie Lovisa, waiting their turn for a hug. Olof's four girls came running, each hoping for a hug from Tobias. They were disappointed when Olof yelled, "Children! Come inside now!"

Anna, Brita, Kajsa and Stina dutifully trudged toward the church.

"Go inside and sit with your mamma."

"Ja, Pappa," they chimed together, heads down.

He turned and clapped Emanuel on his back. "See you in there, brother."

"Tack, Olof." It was not lost on Emanuel that Olof did not wait to be standing there when Lovisa entered the church.

"Hej, Manni," Lovisa said as she stood before Emanuel and shook his hand.

"Hej, Lovisa, I am grateful for your presence." Emanuel said, "And for yours, Dárjá, Toby."

Emanuel was reminded of his long-dead brother, Pehr, when he shook Tobias's hand. The resemblance was remarkable. He held Tobias's shoulder with his left hand as he shook his right hand.

"How is the army treating you, Toby?"

"Well," Tobias responded, "tack, sir!"

"You are a man now, Toby, and an equal," Emanuel said. "You may call me Manni, if you like."

"Tack, sir, ahh, Manni."

"Go find yourselves seats; I hope you can come to the house afterwards?"

"Ja, we will be there, tack, Manni," Lovisa said as she led her children into the church. Heads turned and conversation hushed as they walked into the church. Although Lovisa was a well-respected midwife, and indeed had presided at many of their births, there was an air of awkwardness with her presence here. That was short-lived after several of the older ladies stood and greeted her as she passed. As more and more people smiled or nodded to her and her children as they walked down the aisle, the awkwardness lifted and the chattering continued.

"That was strange!" Dárjá whispered as they took their seats behind Katarina.

"Hej, Lovisa." Katarina turned to look back at them. "Dárjá, Toby."

"Hej, Katarina," Lovisa responded. "How have you been? It

seems we only see each other at funerals."

"Ja, Olof is still being an ass!" Katarina whispered.

Dárjá and Tobias gaped at her and Lovisa had to suppress her giggle.

"Hej, Lovisa, Katarina," Erik Kiällberg greeted as he walked by them with his wife, Kerstin.

"Hej, Erik, Kerstin."

Erik nodded to Dárjá and Tobias, who stifled a salute halfway up, and then nodded to the corporal. This was not lost on Erik, who grinned and winked at Tobias, eliciting a huge grin in return.

The pastor, Yarl Silfersköld, a tall, thin man who had gone to war with the Västerbotten Regiment during the Pomeranian War, presided over the service. He had a great deal of respect for veterans of that war, Emanuel, Olof and Erik, being just a few of those veterans in attendance. He spoke of Emanuel's trials in the war, Sigrid looking after his croft during that time and giving him many children, some called home to God as infants.

After the service and burial, the gathered family and close friends, along with the pastor and his wife, made their way to Emanuel's home. Beside the cottage was his and Erik's sawmill near the village of Brattby. It was not a short journey, so they had planned to stay overnight because much food and alcohol would be consumed. Some of the Sámi families had brought extra lavvus [tents] for people to sleep in and a feast of reindeer and moose meat to their friend's home.

The crowd, close to a hundred people, gathered in Emanuel's yard. The Sámi somehow knew the precise time when everyone would arrive. They had made extra tables and benches with sawn lumber from the mill and had the feast cooked and ready on the long tables. Emanuel looked around, bewildered at the number of people and food before him. Lovisa sidled up to him and commented, "Siggy would be in heaven, feeding all these people!"

"She is in heaven," Emanuel responded, "and, yes, you are right. She would have loved this."

"Ja, sorry," Lovisa said. "She is in heaven, with her children."

"Tack for being here, Lovisa," Emanuel said. "It means a lot to me and my barn [children]."

"Of course, Manni, you are my brother, and Sigrid was my sister." The Radermans long ago took Lovisa in when she walked away from her home after her drunken father, Öhn Larsson, struck her. But long before that, Lovisa and Emanuel's brother, Pehr, were inseparable since they were small children. Back then, Lovisa spent as much time at the Radermans as she did at her own home, even referring to Pehr's parents, Olaus Raderman and his wife, Anna, both deceased now, as Pappa and Mamma.

"Well then, come, sister. Let's go eat!" Emanuel said.

After the meal was finished, and the pastor and his wife left, the akvavit was poured. The pastor's wife, Camilla, looked back longingly as they rode away. "Try this drink, Manni!" Juho said, lifting a jug onto the table in front of him. Juho and Hugo were men of the hunt in the Sámi clan, and life partners, accepted and respected by all in the clan.

"Is that Antte's recipe, Juho?" Emanuel asked with a raised eyebrow.

"Ja, but I have further refined it, my friend!"

Emanuel looked at Juho's partner and asked, "Is it safe, Hugo"

"In small doses, my friend, in small doses."

"Ahh, okay, Juho, I will try some of your hide tanner."

"Hide tanner!" cried Juho. "I will forgive your insult, only because I have so much respect for you!"

"And I you, old friend," Emanuel said, raising his cup. "Skål!"

"Skål!" came the reply.

And that is about where Emanuel's memory of the evening ended. He woke the next day with a head that felt like someone pounded a spike through it. He had somehow made it to his bed the night before, and as he lay there willing the stabbing pain behind his eyes to cease, he could hear many children shrieking and laughing outside. He reeked of something unidentifiable, and urine. When the pain subsided to a dull throb, he rolled over and sat up. He was blinded with renewed pain and a wave of nausea rolled through him. Grabbing the chamber pot, he vomited an acidic mixture of bile and fragments of his last meal.

"You're up!" Lovisa said, entering the room. "It's about time. I feared you were in a coma from that vile poison Juho brought!"

"I am sore all over. What did I do last night?" Emanuel mumbled with a cottonmouth.

"You, mean, aside from dancing on the tables?" Lovisa asked, "or falling off them?"

Emanuel groaned as flashbacks began to slowly emerge.

"Or perhaps singing with Juho, arms around each other like lovers?" Lovisa laughed. "The two of you were mumbling as if your tongues were swelled! Nobody could understand a word either of you were saying, but you two seemed to understand each other, laughing at the same time and all. It was hilarious to watch!"

"Oh, God!" Emanuel groaned, "Do not tell me any more!"

"Ahh, but it is fun, Manni!" Lovisa cried, grinning ear to ear, "like when you tried to pee in the bushes and then started back-peddling until you fell on your back, piss arcing in the air from your exposed little cuk and landing on your face!"

"Oh, God, Lovisa, you are really enjoying this, aren't you?"

"Ja, it is something I will never forget, nor will everyone else!"

Emanuel was about to say something, but then grabbed the chamber pot and spewed another stream of hot vomit.

"God damn, Manni, I did not think you could stink any worse and then you do that!" Lovisa cried, covering her nose. "I will go heat water for a bath."

When Lovisa called him into the kitchen, the copper bathtub was in the center of the room, full of steaming water. "Here, drink this and then get in the tub," she commanded. "This is called soap," she said sarcastically, handing him the soap Sigrid had made from ashes and lard. "Use it and there's clean clothes on the chair," she said on her way out of the cabin. Emanuel only had to remove his long johns as that's all he had on when he woke up. Another groan as another memory flashed in his mind. This one involved him trying to do a jig, Russian style squatting with arms crossed while kicking his feet out, and falling over a bench. That may have been the end of his night because after that, he only recalled flashes of looking up at four Sámi, and the stars above them, each gripping a limb and carrying him through the yard.

He drank tentatively from the steaming cup Lovisa left him. It was a strong, black liquid that seemed to have a positive effect on his condition. The taste took a little getting used to, but by the time he finished the drink, it began to taste pretty good. After the bathwater got cold, Emanuel got up, dried himself off and dressed in clean clothes. He winced when the sunlight seared his eyes as he stepped out of the cabin onto his porch. Immediately, cheers and clapping erupted from the guests still gathered in the yard. Olof called, "Give us a dance, Manni!" much to the glee of everyone. Emanuel was stunned to see the sun high in the sky.

"How long did I sleep?" he asked no one in particular.

"Since the midnight hour to now, midday!" someone called, eliciting scattered chuckles.

"Your boyfriend, Juho, left this morning," Jonas said. "Hugo was very upset with him. They may divorce!" Jonas was Emanuel's only other living brother, other than Olof and, of course, Pehr, although they did not know if Pehr was dead or alive.

Emanuel groaned again as the others brayed laughter.

"Lovisa, what was that drink you gave me?"

"Coffee," Lovisa answered. "We traded for it in Norge last winter. Did you like it?"

"Ja, it was very good and it made me feel better!"

"I will make you some more with the evening meal," Lovisa said, "if you feel like eating by then."

"I don't know, but I will have some more of your coffee, regardless."

Chapter 4
The Sámi Incident

Two days after the funeral, Lovisa and Dárjá rode along the trail that would take them back to the Sámi summer pasture near Storuman. The trail's origin has been lost to history. It was about 8 feet wide and bordered on both sides with poplar trees and willow. Because the trail was seldom used, long grass and willows threaten to take the trail back. Lovisa wondered if the Sámi ever stopped coming to their summer pasture, would the trail disappear? Probably, but for now, several farmers in the area still used the trail to trade with the Sámi.

It would not be long before the Sámi moved to their winter pasture near the coast of Norway. Most of them had left Emanuel's home early the morning after the funeral. Juho and Hugo left later that morning and did not make it as far before stopping to camp. Lovisa and Dárjá rode past their cold campsite at midday on their first day's travel.

"Juho and Hugo didn't make it too far before stopping," Dárjá observed.

"Nej, you can see where Juho got sick."

"Ja, I never saw two men drink so much in one sitting as Manni and Juho!" Dárjá said.

"I thought they were going to kiss at one point," Lovisa said.

"What?" Dárjá asked, then burst out laughing, seeing the grin on her mother's face. They laughed until tears flowed, and then laughed some more.

"Let's move on, Dárjá," Lovisa said when they recovered. "We will camp where the others stopped."

The others, being Sámi, left a lavvu standing for them when they left the day before, along with firewood and kindling. It was appreciated by Lovisa and Dárjá as they arrived late in the day. They saw where Juho and Hugo stopped for a rest before moving on. Lovisa wondered if they considered camping here, but it was probably still early in the day when they passed this place.

"This is very considerate of the people to leave this for us," Dárjá observed.

"Ja, that is our way."

"Do you think Pappa will get better?" Dárjá asked as they made the fire.

"I don't know, Dárjá," Lovisa answered. "I've seen this before and it only gets worse."

"Why do people get this, this illness, Mamma?"

"I wish I knew, min älskling [my darling]," Lovisa said, "but more importantly, I wish I knew how to fix it!"

"Tell me about Pehr, Mamma."

Lovisa was taken aback by the request, but, after thinking about it, decided to tell her.

"Pehr was the love of my life, from the time we were small children to the day he left for war."

"What about Pappa? Don't you love him too?"

"Of course, I do, but Pehr was my first love."

"He is Toby's dad?"

"Ja, he was." Lovisa said, "Do you remember meeting him on the Viking trail when you were small?"

"What?" Dárjá asked, stunned. "I met him?"

"Ja, you and Toby. Pehr was injured and being chased by the

army."

"Why was he being chased by the army?"

"They thought he deserted, but they drove him away — threatened to shoot him for desertion when all he did was lose his memory after being shot in the head by the Prussians."

"That's terrible ... wait, was he that man with the funny eye and bandages wrapped around his chest?"

"Ja, he went through a lot before they caught up to him and shot him."

"They shot him?" Dárjá asked, "After he was injured so bad?"

"Ja, they did, the soldiers."

"How did he get injured?"

"Some bad men attacked him, but he killed them. Then a bear attacked his horse, and he killed the bear with his knife."

"What?" Dárjá cried, "That's amazing!"

"Ja, he was not the strongest of men, but he was tough, like his brother, Jakob." Lovisa said, "That bear hide on Toby's bed was the bear he killed."

"Really?" Dárjá asked. "It's huge! Wait, I remember when you skinned it after meeting that man, Pehr, I mean."

"Ja, and now it is time for bed, min älskling!"

"Mamma, who is Jakob?"

"Jakob was Pehr's older brother; he idolized him," Lovisa said. "Jakob was killed in the same battle where Pehr was shot."

"I wish I knew them, Mamma."

"You know Pehr, through Toby. He is a lot like him."

The next morning, they ate some dried reindeer meat and berry paste before packing up the lavvu. They tied the poles to Dárjá's saddle and then tied the hides between the poles, above the ground, and far enough behind the horse to avoid its droppings. The horse, like all Sámi horses, was used to pulling the travois-like load. They had been traveling at a steady pace for most of the morning before they spotted signs of trouble. The area had some stone outcroppings and sandy patches. They could see Hugo and Juho's tracks, overlaying the tracks of others that went before them. All of a sudden, Lovisa saw a disturbance of tracks. The sand here was churned up and Lovisa had to dismount to determine what happened.

"What is it, Mamma?" Dárjá asked from atop her horse. She used the height to scan the bush on either side of the trail for any sign of danger.

"The main group of people passed without incident, but it looks like Hugo and Juho were attacked," Lovisa said, studying the confusion of prints, "and there's blood."

"Oh, no!" Dárjá whispered, sliding a knife out of her saddlebag.

"Dárjá, I want you to stay here and keep a lookout," Lovisa said. "I am going to follow these drag marks."

"Okay," Dárjá replied, then asked, "Mamma?"

"Ja?'

"Take your knife and don't go too far."

"Ja, I fear what I am going to find."

Lovisa followed the drag marks for about twenty yards and could see a mound covered with leaves up ahead. She looked around and, when she was satisfied no person or animal was nearby, approached the mound after picking up a fallen branch. She poked the mound and could see clothing under the leaves. There was no reaction to her prodding so she began brushing the leaves aside with the branch. It wasn't long before she recognized Juho's clothing. Juho's face was unrecognizable; it looked like he had been savagely beaten until no features were discernible anymore. Some of his clothes were ripped off and she could see where portions of his buttocks were torn off. The bite marks were not from an animal. Gagging, Lovisa fought the rising bile and took several deep breaths before it passed.

She covered the body with leaves and branches and made a tripod over the body as a marker, tying the top with hide string.

"It's Juho; he's dead," Lovisa said when she got back to the trail.

"Oh, no! Poor Juho. What happened?" Dárjá asked, both frightened and sad.

"Someone killed him," Lovisa said. "Someone wearing moccasins."

The statement needed no further explanation; whoever did this was probably Sámi.

"Do you think it was Hugo?" Dárjá asked, eyes huge.

"Nej, see where he ran off?" Lovisa pointed at his tracks, "and see the moccasin prints where someone ran and jumped up?"

"Ja, I see it now, where they struggled and the blood."

"There are blood drops where Hugo's horse ran," Lovisa observed. "I think Hugo was hurt bad. He would not leave Juho otherwise."

"Nej, he wouldn't," Dárjá said, "but look at the moccasin tracks. They follow Hugo's horse and then come back here, where he drags Juho into the bush."

"You are right, Dárjá!" Lovisa said, impressed with her daughter's observation despite the situation. "See how the moccasin toes dig in? The attacker is running hard after Hugo."

"Oh!" Dárjá said, shaken. "What do we do, Mamma?"

"We need to follow the tracks and help Hugo if we can,"

Lovisa said. "Drop the poles and lavvu; we need to ride fast."

They did not have to ride far before they came upon Hugo. He was much in the same condition as Juho, minus the bite marks. He was dragged a little way off the trail and covered with leaves.

"What do we do, Mamma?" Dárjá asked, a tremor in her voice.

"We ride home and warn the people," Lovisa answered, "but we keep a close watch on our surroundings, in case he is still around."

"His tracks lead south, through the bush."

"Ja, good eye, Dárjá," Lovisa acknowledged. "Let's ride hard then. We shouldn't see him unless he circles around, but these tracks are not that old."

And ride hard they did. Whether it was from fear, or the need to warn the others, it is not known. But it was probably a little of both. They came upon Hugo and Juho's horses grazing in an open meadow. Lovisa whistled to them, and the loose horses galloped after them. It was dusk when they rode into the Sámi camp, Hugo and Juho's horses trotting behind them.

They rode past Hugo and Juho's lavvu where Jager and Raul, the Sámi's Karelian bear dogs, lay. They lifted their heads when Lovisa and Dárjá rode by and, not seeing their masters, whined and put their muzzles back down on their forelegs, patiently waiting. Hugo and Juho, with their dogs, were in charge of chasing wolves, bears and other predators away from the people's reindeer herd. Jager and Raul were offspring of Alv, one of Hugo and Juho's original bear dogs. The dogs were fearsome creatures on the hunt, but docile and affectionate in camp, often playing with the children.

"Go find your father, Dárjá!" Lovisa ordered. "I need to find the elders."

Lovisa found them where they usually were, at the elder's fire, pretending to discuss matters of importance, but really just rehashing old heroic deeds and complaining about the laziness of the young.

"Hugo and Juho have been killed!" Lovisa declared without preamble.

"What?" Válde, the leader of the camp, asked. He was elected camp elder after the death of the long-serving leader, Antte. "What is that you say, Gaetki Jägare [Wolverine Hunter]?" He rarely called her Lovisa. Instead, he preferred to show respect by calling her by her Sámi title. She had killed a gaetki with just a walking stick many years ago as it was attacking one of the camp's reindeer.

"Hugo and Juho are dead; Dárjá and I found their bodies on the trail from Brattby," Lovisa said. "Their heads were bashed in and Juho was partly eaten."

"By wolves?"

"Nej, by a man," Lovisa hesitated, "a man who wore moccasins," she added.

"Nej!" they breathed. "A Sámi did this?"

"Mamma!" Dárjá whispered from behind her.

"Come forth, little one!" Válde commanded.

Dárjá stepped forward and stood beside Lovisa. Although in her twenty-fifth year, Válde still occasionally called her 'little one,' with affection.

"What is it, Dárjá?" asked Válde.

"Pappa is gone."

"Ja, he got very upset when you two didn't come home when you said you would," Válde said. "He was screaming and throwing things around in your lavvu, and then he stormed out of camp, ranting like a lunatic; hasn't been seen since."

They all went silent, looking at each other, thinking the same thing.

"We will send the hunters out to track this killer, and to bring Hugo and Juho home," Válde ordered. "Lovisa, you will show our hunters where to find them?"

"Ja, I will."

"You leave in the morning, before sunup; take their dogs with you," Válde said. "Two men will accompany you back with the bodies. The rest will track this killer and some men will stay here to protect the camp."

"I will accompany the trackers, Válde!" Lovisa said.

Válde looked at her and then came to a decision. "It is so."

"Me too," Dárjá said.

"Nej, Dárjá, you will stay here at camp!" Válde said firmly, and then more compassionately, "Where you are needed."

"Ja, Elder Válde," she said with her head bowed.

The next morning before dawn, eight men and Lovisa rode out of the Sámi camp, trailed by Jager and Raul. Lovisa had brought them food before it got dark the night before, but they refused to eat until she sat with them and provided them some comfort. She wondered if these two ferocious, and protective, hunting dogs knew their masters were dead. Now, they stayed close to Lovisa, possibly because Hugo and Juho's scent was on her from when she found them.

They came upon Hugo first. Some ravens were tearing at his flesh and the Sámi men chased them away. They wrapped Hugo in hides as Jager and Raul watched, whining occasionally. They left the body bound tightly on the trail, meaning to pick it up on the way back. Jager and Raul stayed with their dead master until Lovisa coaxed them to come. Their discipline overcame their grief as they slowly rose and followed Lovisa.

When they got near the site of Juho's body, Lovisa raised her hand and signaled for a bow. Miku handed her his bow and an arrow. She knocked the arrow, drew the bowstring back, aimed and let loose the arrow. The others didn't see what she shot at until they walked up to the body and saw a wolverine with an arrow through its heart lying behind the body.

"It was time," Lovisa said. "People were forgetting I'm a gaetki jägare."

Despite the grim situation, they all grinned and clapped her shoulder in turn. The wolverine had fed on Juho, taking up where the killer left off, destroying the evidence of cannibalism.

"Are you sure, Lovisa, that it was human bite-marks and not a gaetki's?" one of them asked.

"Ja, I am sure, no doubt."

"Okay, let's wrap Juho and take him home." Two men placed Hugo and Juho on the two travois they brought with them and took them back to camp.

Lovisa tied the wolverine onto one of their horses. "Take this to the tanning lavvu."

The man nodded respectfully before mounting and riding off.

"Lovisa, do you think you can get Jager and Raul on the killer's trail?"

"I will try, Miku."

It took some coaxing, but the dog's instincts took over when Lovisa took them to the moccasin tracks. They snuffled around, circling and going back, before bolting in the direction the tracks were heading, baying as they went.

"We need to follow on foot," Lovisa said. "The horses won't make it through that brush."

"Okay, Nikko, you and Jan take the horses and follow the baying as best you can," Miku ordered. "We will meet up again before nightfall." Lovisa, Miku and the three other Sámi hunters took off at a run, crashing through the brush, following the dog's path.

By early evening, they had covered several miles, more or less in a straight line. The route the killer led them on was through swamps and areas of blown down trees they had to climb over. They were covered in nettles and burdocks when they emerged back onto the trail.

"I think I know where he is heading," Lovisa said.

"Where?" Miku asked.

"To Toby's croft."

"Then it is Dánel."

"We do not know that, Miku," Lovisa said more sternly than she meant to.

"Ja, you are right." Miku said, "Call the dogs back, Lovisa."

The next few minutes were a cacophony of dog whistles and shouts meant for the horsemen. The dogs arrived first, excited and eager to continue, but resigning themselves to the order to stay. They kept close to Lovisa. The men removed as much of the nettles and burdocks as they could while they waited for the horsemen to arrive. Lovisa picked the burdocks from the dogs when she was finished with her own. The horsemen arrived an hour later, having to go around a large swamp.

Chapter 5
Brattby

While the Sámi were chasing a killer, Emanuel and Erik were back at work sawing lumber. Erik knew Emanuel wanted to keep busy, to push thoughts of Sigrid to the back of his mind, at least for a little while. Erik's wife, Kerstin, was staying at the sawmill during the daytime to help with the children. Erik and Kerstin were never able to have children; they didn't know why, but accepted it as God's will.

They sat on a stack of fresh-cut lumber, taking a break and drinking water from enamel cups. They would scoop a wooden pail of water from the river and place it in the shade covered with a wooden lid to keep the sawdust out. Emanuel sighed and thought that he would never tire of the smell of fresh-cut spruce and pine.

"You see him?" Erik whispered.

"Ja, he showed up about ten minutes ago, just crouched there in the willows watching us."

"Kind of spooky; do you recognize him?"

"Nej," Emanuel said. "Erik, could you tell the children to go inside and stay there with Kerstin?"

"Ja, I will do that."

"Get my pistol and come back here." He was pleased with how easily they both slipped back into combat mode after all the years since the war.

As calmly as he could, Erik walked over to where the children were doing their chores in the barn and pens and ordered them to go inside the cabin in such a stern way, they obeyed without objection. He followed them in and came back out shortly afterward, walking back to the sawmill. Emanuel could see the bulge of his pistol under his shirt, hoping the watcher wouldn't notice it. He stood and stretched as Erik approached him.

"I will go get my musket and flank him," Emanuel said. "Try to keep his attention without being obvious."

"Okay, your musket is loaded; on the porch, leaning against the door sill."

"Tack, Erik."

They both felt the thrill of impending battle. Emanuel was surprised that he missed that feeling as he walked nonchalantly to his cabin. Hidden from the watcher's view, Emanuel glanced at the cabin's windows as he grabbed his musket and saw seven frightened faces looking out at him. He grinned and winked at them before running to the bush, keeping the cabin between himself and the watcher. Over the years, Emanuel and Erik had cleared the land and thinned it of the largest millable trees and knew every square foot of the area. He ran straight for a long, low granite outcropping, then ran at a crouch for a distance behind it until he passed within thirty yards of the watcher's position across a small slough. He crept to the top of the outcropping and carefully peered over the top. He could see the watcher's position, but a thick willow growth hid him from view. The watcher chose his position well. The only approach obstructed from his view was through the slough, which would give him ample warning of attack. With no other option, Emanuel attached his bayonet and, after taking a deep breath, charged over the hill and splashed through the slough, letting loose the Västerbottens

Regiment's battle cry as he went. Erik, hearing that, followed suit, letting loose his battle cry and charging across the sawmill yard directly at the watcher. Of course, the Västerbotten's battle cry was the same as any other regiment's, but they liked to think it was their own.

Erik arrived a few seconds after Emanuel, who was standing near the spot where the watcher had crouched, soaked from the charge through the slough's brackish water. There was no one in sight.

"Skit, did you see him leave, Erik?"

"Nej, he is like a ghost!" Erik panted, "He was there and when we charged, just disappeared like a wisp of smoke!"

"Well, he was definitely here. Look at his tracks."

"Should we try to follow him?"

"Nej, I do not want to leave my children alone while he is out here somewhere."

"Ja, let's get back there," Erik said, a sudden urgency in his voice.

"That was exhilarating, though!" Emanuel said with a grin.

"Ja!" They both laughed nervously as the adrenalin rush began to dissipate.

They walked into the cabin and were barraged by five children and Kerstin demanding to know what was going on, and one screaming infant.

"Quiet!" boomed Emanuel, and in a quieter voice, "Kerstin, could you quieten Barbro?"

"Ja, but then I want to know what is going on!"

After calm was restored, Emanuel explained about the mysterious watcher. He went on to describe how they had scared him off.

"I don't think that man will be back after the sight of two old soldiers screaming the regiment's battle cry and charging with weapons drawn right at him!"

Erik laughed, "Nej, I say with some certainty that he is probably changing out of soiled trousers right now!"

The children all laughed at this, but it still warranted a withering glare from Kerstin, until she too had to laugh nervously. The laughter died suddenly when eight-year-old Maria screamed and pointed at one of the windows. Emanuel and Erik both caught a glimpse of a wild man's face looking in at them before ducking out of sight. They grabbed their weapons and charged out of the cabin into the early evening twilight.

"There!" Erik pointed at a figure entering the bush.

Emanuel raised his musket and fired without hesitation at the fleeing figure. The musket's report brought a fresh round of screams from the cabin. Young Olaus came running out of the cabin holding Emanuel's army sword. Emanuel looked at him, hesitated and then nodded. "Come on, son. Let's go get him!" The three of them ran toward where they last saw the man, Erik glancing back in time to see Kerstin shutting the cabin's door. He had no doubt she would barricade the door and protect Manni's children with her life.

There was just enough daylight left when they reached the bush line for them to look for signs of the intruder.

"Look, Manni!" Erik said, indicating blood on a birch sapling's leaf.

"Good, I hit the bastard!" Emanuel said with satisfaction. "Let's get back to the cabin; we will track him tomorrow in the daylight."

"Nej, Manni," Erik said. "I will track him; you stay with your family in case he circles back."

Emanuel thought on it, then said, "Maybe you are right, Erik."

"I want to go with Erik in the morning, Father!" Olaus pleaded.

Emanuel looked at his thirteen-year-old son, almost a man, and said, "You were brave just now, Olaus and if Erik will have you, you can go with him."

"Can I, Erik?" Olaus asked.

"Olaus, I would be proud to fight beside you!"

Olaus puffed out his narrow chest and beamed at the praise. Emanuel was worried he might burst. Olaus ran ahead to brag to his siblings as they headed back to the cabin.

"Who did that look like, Manni, the face in the window?"

"Dánel," Emanuel replied. "But I am not sure. This was a wild man, like some of the soldiers who went mad at Pommern [Pomerania]."

"Ja, you're right, out of their minds with that wild-eyed look to them."

"I am worried about Lovisa and Dárjá," Emanuel said. "I think I will take everyone in the wagon tomorrow morning and go see Toby."

"Ja, that is good, Manni."

"Tack för den här dagen [Thank you for this day], comrade," Emanuel said, shaking Erik's hand. They shook as soldiers, grasping each other's forearm.

The wagon ride to Tobias Öhn's croft was uneventful, other than the constant chatter, hair pulling and laughter of five energetic children. Once in the wagon and moving on the open road, they quickly forgot about the wild man. But not Emanuel and Kerstin. Emanuel was watchful while Kerstin was obviously worried about Olaus.

"He's just a boy!" she whispered to Emanuel.

"You forget; Erik went to war when he was a year younger than Olaus," Emanuel said, touched that she cared so deeply for his children, "and he fought better than most soldiers, I'll say."

"Tack, Manni," she said with a sigh.

They rode into Tobias's farmyard in the early afternoon, having stopped numerous times for toilets. Emanuel went with the children to a discrete spot behind willows. With his back turned to the child doing his or her business, he would scan the surrounding bush for danger. He had to grin as each of his girls would say, "Don't look, Pappa" as they finished up.

Tobias was on the roof of his cabin, replacing some sod that had washed through in thin spots when they arrived at his farm.

"Välkommen, Manni, Kerstin, little trolls!"

"Hej, Toby!" came the reply from Emanuel and Kerstin, yells and shrieks from the children. They loved their uncle Tobias, especially eight-year-old Maria who, along with her cousins, Kajsa and Stina, secretly vowed to marry him when they grew up. Tobias inherited Lovisa's blonde hair and blue eyes and Pehr's handsome features. He was built slight, like his parents, but he had a toughness about him that larger men sensed and respected.

"I'll be right down," he called. "Go inside and make yourselves at home."

"Tack, Toby!" Kerstin said, walking to the porch with little Barbro in hand.

"You kids stay in the yard and don't wander off!" Emanuel told the other children forcefully. This provoked a look of puzzlement from Tobias.

"What is it, Manni?" Tobias asked after he climbed down his ladder. There was one birch sapling rung missing, forcing him to jump the last few feet to the ground.

"Last night, Erik and I spotted someone watching us from the bush line behind our sawmill."

"Nej!" Tobias asked, "Who was it?"

"We couldn't tell from that distance, so we got our weapons and charged his position, but he disappeared into the woods."

"That is strange. Is everyone okay?"

"Ja," Emanuel replied. "But then, when we were all sitting in the cabin, he looked in through a window!"

"Nej!"

"Ja, it is true!"

"What did you do, Manni?"

"Erik and I ran out and chased after him," Emanuel said. "I took a shot at him as he was entering the woods."

"Really, you shot at him!"

"Ja, he was a wild man, Toby!" Emanuel said, "And a threat to my children!"

"Of course; you did right."

"But Toby," Emanuel hesitated. "Erik and I both agree that he looked an awful lot like Dánel."

"Nej!" Toby breathed, not hiding his shock and then anger at the suggestion.

"Ja, it looked like him, but it was hard to tell for sure, with the hair hanging in his face and those wild eyes."

Tobias's anger left him as he looked at his uncle.

"You should go see your sister and mother; make sure they are safe," Emanuel said.

"Ja, of course," Tobias said, heading into his cabin.

"And Toby?"

"Ja?" Tobias stopped on his porch and turned to him.

"Take your weapons and be watchful. This man is like a ghost."

Tobias nodded and walked into the cabin.

Emanuel was outside, keeping a close watch on his children when Tobias came out of his cabin, wearing his sword and carrying his musket and field bag. He saddled his horse and galloped out of the yard without acknowledging Emanuel or the children. Kerstin came out onto the porch and said to Emanuel, "He told us to stay overnight and to help ourselves to food."

"Ja, that is good," Emanuel replied. "It would be dark by the time we got back to the mill."

Chapter 6
Tobias

Tobias started out riding hard, but then realized he had to pace himself or his horse would suffer. He slowed to a trot and kept watch of his surroundings and the trail ahead, searching the dirt for tracks. The ride to the Sámi summer pasture would take two days. He noted the leaves were turning and some had already fallen. It wouldn't be long before the people left for their winter pasture in Norway. He arrived late in the day, on his second day, to a strangely quiet camp. He was challenged by herdsmen, who then quickly recognized him. "Hej, Toby, Välkommen!"

"Hej," Tobias replied. "What news have you?"

"There are strange things happening, my friend!"

"Tell me!"

"I am not told these things, Toby," the herdsman said. "You should ask Válde. He knows all."

"Tack, my friend," Tobias said. He would ask Válde, but first, he needed to check on his mother.

Her lavvu was empty, in shambles, so he headed for the tanning lavvu. She was not there either, but was told Dárjá was with Florá. Florá was Dárjá's grandmother, mother to Dánel. She was in declining health, bedridden for the most part. Tobias called Dárjá from the lavvu's door flap.

"Come in, Toby!"

"What is happening, Dárjá? No one will tell me."

Dárjá told Tobias everything that happened, starting with finding Juho and Hugo, and ending with Lovisa and the hunters going out to track the killer. Florá was waving her arm from her pallet, beckoning them closer.

"It is not Dánel!" she rasped. "My boy would not do that!" The effort took a lot out of her and she flopped back down, exhausted.

"Nej, of course, it's not Pappa," Dárjá said.

After a few moments, Florá drifted off to sleep and Dárjá motioned Tobias outside.

They walked a little way from the lavvu when they heard excited voices from the edge of camp.

"What now?" Dárjá said, exasperated. They ran to where a crowd was gathering around two men on horseback. They found an opening among the crowd and saw the bundles.

"It's Juho and Hugo's bodies," she whispered to Tobias.

"Dárjá!" one of them called from atop his horse, "your mother, Gaetki Jägare, has killed another one!" He made a show of raising the wolverine carcass in the air to much oohs and aahs, despite the solemnity of the bodies draped over the horses. Dárjá stepped forward and accepted the animal, struggling with its weight.

"Is my mamma alright?"

"Ja, she is with the hunters, chasing the killer!" The man had a sense of the dramatic and his declaration had the intended effect, eliciting cheers and slaps on Dárjá's back. Dárjá handed the wolverine to Tobias and they made their way to the tanning lavvu.

"They didn't slap me on the back!" Tobias grumbled.

"Some feel you betrayed the people when you left the camp

to join the Swedish army."

"Some?" Tobias said. "Most, you mean."

"I'm sorry, Toby. I don't know what to say."

"It's okay; let's get this gaetki to the lavvu," Tobias said, and after thinking about it, added, "Who will skin it?"

"I will."

"Ja, it is good." Tobias said, "I am going after them."

"I know," Dárjá sighed. "Be careful, brother."

* * * *

Tobias switched horses and rode out of the camp, following the route the hunters had taken. He was still a member of the clan and the horses belonged to all the people. It was a different route than he came on, this one heading due east toward the Umeå River and Brattby. The trail to Tobias's farm was on a more southeasterly route. The hunter's trail was easy to follow, even after they left the trail, due to the number of horses they had. He did not notice where some had gone on foot through the thick brush. He decided to make camp when twilight made it hard to follow the tracks. Reasoning that since the hunters had the killer on the run, it would be safe to build a fire for cooking and heat. Even after the events of the last few days, Tobias slept soundly.

After decamping in the morning, he continued down the trail, following the hunter's tracks. By midday, he found where the hunters had veered off, heading in a direct line that Tobias knew would eventually take them to the trail to his farm. He also noted they had Jager and Raul with them. He had forgotten about the bear dogs and felt better knowing they were with his mother. Heading out at a gallop, he made quick time, increasing his speed once on the trail. The horse tracks led him straight to his farm.

Arriving at his home the next day, he could see where the hunters had searched every corner of his farm. Puzzled, Tobias sat on his porch, in the rocking chair that he had found in the small barn's loft when he was first assigned the croft. He found it conducive to deep thought. He even considered taking up the pipe, but had not an opportunity to buy one yet. In his mind's eye, the image of himself sitting on his rocking chair, puffing his pipe, would portray a man of deep wisdom, or so he thought. Getting back to the task at hand, he wondered why they would search his farm so thoroughly. Did they think his stepfather was hiding here? And why was he now thinking of Dánel as his stepfather instead of as his father, after calling him father all his life? So much to think about, Tobias thought, standing up and shaking his head. He figured he ought to tend to his chickens before taking up the hunter's trail again. After spreading some grain for the clucking chickens, he mounted his horse just as the searchers rode into his yard.

"Hej, Toby," Lovisa called. "I was worried when you weren't here."

"Hej, Mamma," Tobias answered. "Emanuel, Kerstin and the children came here to warn me about a wild man on the loose. I went to the summer pasture to make sure you and Dárjá were safe."

"Is Dárjá safe? What did they say about the wild man?"

"Put up your horses and come inside," Tobias told the assembled Sámi hunters. "I will tell you all I know."

After unsaddling his own horse, Tobias went into his cabin, lit the fire and hung a kettle full of water on the hanger. He had gathered over a dozen eggs from his hen house and was going to boil them for his guests. After they found seats, Tobias told them what Emanuel had told him.

"He is sure it was Dánel?" Lovisa asked.

"Nej, not sure, but I think it was him."

"Why do you say that, Toby?"

"It all fits. First he goes crazy when you and Dárjá are gone longer than expected." He held up a finger, indicating for her to wait when she started to interject. "Then Hugo and Juho are found dead; moccasin tracks indicating a Sámi likely did the killing. The only Sámi unaccounted for at the time is Dánel. Then Manni, Erik, and Kerstin all say the wild man that looked in their window resembled Dánel."

Lovisa sat back, clearly struck by Tobias's analysis, then buried her face in her hands. The Sámi hunters were clearly uncomfortable, not sure what they should do. Tobias saved them by going around the table and kneeling beside his mother. Tobias held Lovisa as all her grief and fears let loose in shuddering sobs. The hunters could hear Jager and Raul whining on the porch and scratching on the door. One of the Sámi looked at Tobias, who nodded. The hunter stood and went to the door, opening it and letting the dogs rush in. They ran straight to Lovisa, Jager going so far as to push between Tobias and Lovisa. She had to smile and scratch their heads, touched by their affection.

"We lost his trail when he entered a creek," Miku said. "We followed it for a mile, but could not see if he left the creek. The dogs lost his scent."

"The creek to the east," Tobias asked, "running north-south?"

"Ja, that is the one."

Tobias looked at Lovisa, comprehension dawning on her.

"That creek runs right by Olof's farm," Tobias said. "It is the other farm Dánel is familiar with, where he met my mamma for the first time, many years ago."

"I will warn Olof!" Tobias declared, grabbing his musket.

"Wait, Toby. Jaari and Kjell will go with you!" Miku said.

The two Sámi men nodded and followed Tobias out of the cabin. They saddled their horses, which were clearly put out, having settled in for the night after being rubbed down, fed and watered. Tobias set a fast pace, familiar with the road to the Raderman farm. They thundered into Olof's yard after dark, facing a musket sticking out one window and a pistol out the other. Lanterns were hung about the yard, the same ones used for outdoor celebrations in years gone by.

Tobias and the others skidded to a stop in front of the porch amid a cloud of dust.

"Toby!" Olof called. "I just about shot you!"

"We came to warn you, there is a wild man on the loose!"

"Ja, he was here, stole a chicken from my hen house. Bit the head off it, then ran into the bush laughing like a lunatic!"

"Did you get a good look at him?"

"Nej," Olof hesitated, eying the two Sámi men, "but I found moccasin tracks."

"We think it is Dánel," Tobias said, looking back at Jaari and Kjell for concurrence. "He killed two Sámi men already."

"Nej!" Olof breathed, "How can that be?"

"He has been acting strange, losing his memory, and his temper."

Katarina had come out onto the porch, holding Olof's pistol, pointed up. Four little faces with big eyes looked out the windows.

"I will make a meal," she said, uncocking the pistol and walking back into the cabin.

"I would not want to meet her in battle!" Tobias observed.

"Nej," Olof chuckled, "you would not!"

"Put up your horses in the barn," Olof said to them. "You will stay here tonight."

"Tack," Tobias said, "we can try to pick up his trail in the morning."

After seeing to their horses, Toby, Jaari and Kjell walked into the cabin.

"That smells good, Katarina!" Tobias said.

"Toby!" the four girls shrieked, running to hug him.

Anna and Brita, fourteen and twelve respectfully, had a huge crush on Tobias and pushed and shoved to sit beside him. Kajsa and Stina, ten and nine, just loved Tobias unconditionally.

They dined on ham, turnips, knäckebröd and lingonberry jam. Jaari and Kjell moaned and groaned over the meal, savoring every bite.

"This is the best food I have ever eaten!" Jaari proclaimed.

"Ja, it is!" Kjell agreed, rubbing his belly with a satisfied grin.

Katarina swelled with pride, then horror, as the two Sámi men belched loudly. Seeing Katarina's reaction, Tobias said, "It is a compliment to the cook when a Sámi belches after a meal."

Katarina smiled, but did not look entirely convinced.

"What does a fart mean?" Kajsa asked.

Her mother cried, "Kajsa!"

"But Toby just farted. I heard him. It went 'poof,'" pursing her lips and spreading her fingers in the air.

The entire table burst into laughter, Tobias tousling Kajsa's hair. "I always fart when I eat turnips, little one!"

"Then why do you eat them?" she asked, brushing her hair back with her fingers.

"Because I like to fart!" he said, tousling her hair again, this time with both hands. After the laughter died down, Toby said, "We will sleep in the barn; take turns watching."

"Ja, that is good," Olof said.

"Toby can sleep with us!" Stina said, "Me and Kajsa, he can tell us scary stories!"

"Nej, little one," Tobias said. "You have had enough scares for one night."

This brought a duet of "awws" from Kajsa and Stina.

"And," Tobias said reaching across the table, "I'm going to have some more turnips!"

This time the 'awws' came from Jaari and Kjell, which brought everyone to tears, laughing.

*****

The next morning, after a breakfast of porridge and knäckebröd, which, much to Olof's amusement, Tobias soaked in the porridge to soften, much like Pehr used to do.

"What?" Tobias asked.

"Nothing, Toby, just remembering something from a long time ago," Olof said. "That reminds me. There's something in the barn I want to show you."

They walked to the barn, uncle and nephew.

"It's up there," Olof said, "in the loft."

Tobias was confused. He and the two Sámi had slept up there and there wasn't anything out of the ordinary. He followed Olof up the stairs and stood waiting for Olof to show him what was so important that they were delaying their pursuit.

"Over here." Olof waved for him to follow. He walked over to a corner of the loft and brushed aside some hay, exposing a cloth-covered container. Olof pulled the cloth off and there sat an intricately carved chest.

"This was Pehr's soldier's chest," Olof said huskily. He cleared his throat and said, "Those carvings and joints were made by your mother."

Tobias knelt before the chest and ran his fingers over the carvings, feeling the smooth contours. "It's beautiful," he said quietly.

"Open it up."

Tobias lifted the top and looked inside. Of course, all Pehr's soldier equipment had gone with him to Pomerania. All that was left was an old pair of work shoes and some cooking utensils. He picked up and examined each item, thinking, my father wore these shoes, and My father ate with this fork.

"Tack for showing me this, Olof," Tobias said quietly.

"Nej, Toby, you don't understand," Olof said, putting his hand on Tobias's shoulder. "It is yours. It rightfully belongs to his son."

It took a while before Tobias could answer.

"Tack, Olof."

"It is good. Now go find this killer. You can pick up the chest whenever you like."

* * * *

They found the wild man's trail easily enough, blood and chicken feathers leading the way.

"Jaari, can you take the horses and stay close to us?" Tobias asked. "We will whistle now and then so you know where we are."

"Ja, I will do that."

"Be watchful, my friend, all around, not just in our direction,"

Tobias said.

Kjell and Tobias entered the forest where the tracks led. "Why can't he stick to trails?" Kjell grumbled as nettles attached themselves to his pants.

"Then he wouldn't be crazy," Tobias said.

"I suppose you're right," sighed Kjell.

The tracks did cross the road once, Jaari waiting patiently for them as they emerged from the bush.

"He crossed here and someone else followed him in," Jaari said. "Two men, in shoes."

"Huh," Tobias pondered, "I wonder who that could be?"

"Only one way to find out!" Kjell said.

"Ja," Tobias said. "Jaari, if he continues in this direction, he will cross the road back to the pasture, the way we came."

"Ja?"

"Ride up ahead and find a high spot," Tobias said. "Maybe you can catch him as he crosses the road."

"Okay, that is a good plan."

"And, Jaari?"

"Ja?"

"Don't forget, he has already killed two people."

Jaari nodded and rode out at a gallop, trailing Tobias and Kjell's horses.

"Well," Tobias said, watching Jaari ride away, "you ready?"

"Ja." Kjell sighed and plowed headlong into the bush. They skirted the larger fallen trees. Others they stepped over and some they crawled underneath. The line of travel was dense with burdock and hidden pockets of swamp water. Clouds of mosquitos feasted on their exposed skin until Kjell stopped and covered himself with mud from one of the swamp holes. Tobias quickly followed Kjell's example. They came across an old clearing with what looked like the remnants of ancient building foundations.

"Look, Toby, an old sword!"

"Ach, it is rusted; not much use anymore," Tobias responded.

"Ja, it is huge and looks like it was well made, from what's left of it."

Tobias took it from Kjell's hands, turned it over, inspecting the workmanship of the relic.

"Ja, too bad it is rusted so bad," he said, handing it back to Kjell.

"Ja," sighed Kjell, tossing the sword into a swamp pit where it would continue its disintegration. "I wonder who lived here."

"The people before — the warrior tribes," Tobias responded.

"Ah, I have heard of them, from the elders."

They eventually emerged back on the road leading to the pasture. Waiting for them was Jaari, Erik and Emanuel's boy, Olaus. The sight of Tobias and Kjell, unrecognizable under all the mud and burdocks, gave Olaus a start. He was going to draw his father's sword when Erik stopped him with his hand.

"Hej, Erik, Olaus," Tobias said, nodding at Jaari.

"Hey, Toby."

"Do you know Kjell?"

"Nej, I don't believe so," Erik said.

After introductions were made, Jaari said, "That is Jager and Raul you hear; they had come charging through the bush, followed by Lovisa and Miku, crossing the road with barely a glance our way."

"Let's follow the road west, see if we can parallel the dogs," Erik said. They could hear dogs baying in the distance.

"Ja, that is my thought too," Tobias said as he pulled burdocks off his trousers.

Erik looked at Olaus, who was grinning ear to ear and hopping up and down with excitement.

"Keep your head about you, Olaus," he said to him. "This is a dangerous task we are on."

"Ja, sorry, Erik."

"It's okay. We are glad you are with us," he said, clasping his shoulder and nodding at him, causing Olaus to swell with pride.

They turned at the sound of horses approaching.

Nikko and Jan rode up to their position, trailing two horses.

"Hej, friends," Nikko hailed.

"Hej," came a smattering of replies from the group.

"Have Miku and Lovisa passed this way?" Nikko asked.

"Ja, they crossed here about half an hour ago."

They all were quiet, listening for the baying of dogs. Hearing them to the southwest, Erik said, "We are going to follow along the road. They seem to be running parallel to it."

"Ja, let's go," Nikko said, eager for the chase to continue. More and more leaves were falling, making their view into the bush a little more open. Olaus was clearly enjoying himself, being part of the excitement. He couldn't wait to brag to his friends about it. He enjoyed the crisp, clean mountain air and even the smell of the horses. He decided right then and there that he would join the Swedish army, or maybe the cavalry, as soon as they would have him. He promised himself he would talk with Erik about it whenever he had a moment alone with him.

After trotting the horses for a few miles, they rounded a bend in the road and spotted Lovisa, Miku and the two dogs. They greeted each other and shared recent activities. Miku told them that the dogs nearly had the killer until he ran into a large swamp, going under the surface.

"We stayed and watched for him for a half-hour, then circled it," Miku said. "He never came out."

"He is drowned then?" Jan asked.

"It looks that way. No one can stay under the surface that long and survive."

"Good!" Jan said, "Let the leeches and crabs feast on him!"

Nikko nudged him and nodded toward Lovisa, who stood with her head down. He did not notice the glare he got from Tobias.

"Sorry, Lovisa," Jan muttered. "I wasn't thinking."

Lovisa nodded, but kept her head down. Tobias went to her and they walked off a short distance to grieve Dánel's death.

Two miles away, at the edge of the swamp, a reed moved. Then a head emerged. Dánel stood, dripping putrid water and spat out the reed he had used to breath through when he hid underwater. He began laughing hysterically. After a few moments, he stopped, cleared his throat and looked around. He walked out of the swamp, picking leeches off his body and popping them into his mouth, biting into them and feeling a satisfying burst of blood flooding his mouth.

Chapter 7
Trondheim, Norway

Pehr Olofsson watched his apprentice, Kristian Henrikssen, lay the sole pattern over the leather.

"See the horn blow?" Pehr said, pointing to a barely visible scar on the cowhide most likely from an encounter with a bull's horn. "We must avoid all imperfections, no matter how slight."

Kristian turned the pattern away from the faint scar.

"Nej, Kristian," Pehr said. "A little more, to avoid the tick bite."

Kristian leaned closer and spotted the tiny hole.

"That is not a pore?"

"Nej, it is a tick bite," Pehr said, removing the pattern and lifting the hide up in front of the lantern above the work station. "See the light through the hole?"

Kristian looked, but did not immediately see it. Pehr moved the hide a little and Kristian said, "There, I see it!"

"Our shoes are of the highest quality, none better in all of Norge [Norway]," Pehr said. "We must ensure there are no imperfections, no matter how small."

"Ja, okay, sir. I will be more careful."

Pehr Olofsson was the son of Olof, Olaus to family and friends. Olaus became Soldier Raderman when he joined the army and all his children were born Raderman instead of the typical Olofsson or Olofsdotter.

Pehr's journey began on the Raderman farm in Hössjö,

Sweden. There, he joined the army in 1755 at the age of eighteen and was assigned the name Soldier Rask. A year later, he became engaged to his neighbor and childhood sweetheart, Lovisa Öhn. But before they could marry, Pehr and three of his brothers were called to war in Swedish Pomerania against the Prussian Empire.

During a battle where Pehr's brother, Jakob, was killed, Pehr was hit in the head by a musket ball and presumed dead. After the battle, he was taken prisoner by the Prussians and left on a farm to recuperate and serve out the war as slave labor. The injury caused memory loss, which only returned when the war was ending. When Pehr left the farm, he took the farmer's granddaughter with him, rescuing her from a miserable life with abusive grandparents. When he made his way to the Swedish garrison at Stralsund, the Swedish commander was suspicious that Pehr's memory had returned just as the war was ending. He placed Pehr under arrest for desertion and there was talk of execution the next day. Upon hearing that, Pehr, with the help of his old friend Erik Kiällberg, escaped and made his way to Lübeck in northern Prussia. There, he found a job and learned the craft of shoemaking.

The pull of home became too great and he ventured back to Hössjö, via Trondheim. It was in Trondheim where Pehr was set upon by three brigands, severely beaten, robbed of all his money and left for dead in an alley. He was found by a policeman, Axel Paulsen, and taken to a hospital with life-threatening injuries. After recovering, Pehr was taken into the home of the policeman and his wife, Gunhild, to convalesce. A lingering aftereffect of the beating was a wayward eye; his left eye pointed 45° to the left.

The next unfortunate event in Pehr's journey happened when he was fit enough to venture over the ancient Viking trail into

Sweden. The brigands, three of them, fearing Pehr would relate their identities to the authorities, took after him into the mountains. Pehr killed one, wolves killed another and the third was released to his own devices on the remote trail, his fate unknown. Pehr continued on to Hössjö where he learned both his parents had died and his fiancé had married a Sámi man and started a family.

Heartbroken, he made his way back over the Viking trail. He was pursued by the Swedish army after Lovisa's father had betrayed his presence in Sweden to a Swedish soldier. Pehr's bad luck continued when his horse was killed by a crazed bear, injuring Pehr's ribs in the process. Pehr managed to kill the bear, as it locked onto his horse's neck, by plunging his knife into the bear's head, which didn't have the intended result until Pehr twisted the knife with all his strength.

Stumbling toward the Swedish-Norwegian border, Pehr was shocked to see Lovisa and two children standing on the trail. After a bittersweet reunion, meeting his son for the first time, Pehr continued his journey on a horse Lovisa gave him. Within yards of the border, a Swedish soldier shot Pehr out of his saddle, the musket ball hitting him in the shoulder. But Pehr's luck would change for the better when Axel Paulsen and several Trondheim policemen, who were searching for the brigands, came around a corner of the trail and carried Pehr over the border into Norway and to safety. The Swedish soldiers would report Pehr's death to their regiment commander. They did it to avoid the embarrassment of their failure and also to give a fellow soldier — some had fought with him in the war — a chance at survival by doing so.

In the years since, Pehr lived with the Paulsens, becoming like a son to them. And still thinking he was a fugitive of the Swedish empire, Pehr took the traditional last name of Olofsson in honor of his late father.

With Gunhild's assistance, Pehr was able to straighten his left eye by doing eye exercises, where he would look as far as he could to the right without moving his head, several times a day. The wayward eye eventually moved back into alignment and had not caused him any concerns since.

Pehr then resumed his work as a shoemaker, working at a local shop until he earned enough to present an offer to the owner. His reputation had grown to the point where customers would journey from as far as Oslo to have custom shoes made by him. Pehr had saved his money for two years until he felt he had enough to make a fair offer.

"Why should I sell you my shop when business has never been better?" the owner had asked when Pehr broached the subject.

"Because if you don't, I will open my own shop down the street," Pehr had replied, knowing that he was the only reason the shoemaker's shop was doing so well. In fact, the store was on the verge of closing before Pehr had walked in looking for a job. The owner, getting on in age, had made more money in the two years Pehr had worked for him than in all the other years he had been in business. Knowing his business would again be on the verge of collapse if Pehr left, he accepted the offer and entered into a comfortable retirement.

Pehr, now forty years old, had four employees: three shoemakers, each having apprenticed under his tutelage for a period of three years, and the current apprentice, Kristian. Pehr had classic Swedish features, blonde hair, blue eyes and a boyish grin. As a young man, he had a slight build and an effeminate nature, but years of war and hardships in the aftermath had toughened him physically and mentally. Now an established businessman with a soldier's bearing, Pehr drew many a lady's glance when he walked down the streets of Trondheim.

Although the running of a successful business took up most of his time, Pehr still made the occasional pair of shoes by request, as time would allow, for his most loyal of customers. Even so, he still had to turn away many such requests. But Pehr was now feeling restless; he craved another adventure. What that adventure would be, he hadn't decided yet, but, in the following months, the adventure would come to him.

Chapter 8
September 8, 1777
The Raderman Farm

Three weeks after the killings of Juho and Hugo, things were getting back to normal, or as normal as could be. The Sámi had moved back to their winter pasture in Norway. And for the first time in their lives, the Radermans, as with other families in the region, began securing their doors at night. Almost all, that is, except for Erik Kiällberg. He reasoned that, if someone wanted to come in, they were welcome, and if they were meaning harm to his wife or himself, well then, he would promptly change their minds.

So, it was that Maria Emanuelsdotter was visiting her cousins, Kajsa and Stina Olofsdotter, at the Raderman farm. They were all within two years of age of each other and were very close. Their days were spent doing their chores, playing house, doing each other's hair and hide and seek. And it was while playing hide and seek that the next incident occurred.

The Raderman farm was ideal for hide and seek. There was the barn, a hide and seeker's dream with its loft, stalls, lean-tos and piles of straw and hay. The house itself also offered numerous hiding places such as under the porches, after careful inspection for spiders and rodents, and, inside, with all the rooms plus the loft. Outside, there were trees, pens and the storehouse. So, it was not alarming for the child who was 'it' not to be able to find a hider and it was not uncommon for a hider to stay hidden long after 'it' gave up. And after an hour of being 'it,' Stina was only successful in finding her cousin, Maria. Stina was becoming annoyed at Kajsa for not showing herself after loudly announcing that she was giving up.

Even after Stina recruited Maria in the search, they were unsuccessful in finding Kajsa. Calls of "Kajsa!" echoed throughout the farm until the rest of the family joined in the search. In the second hour, mother Katarina was becoming frantic. Olof made the hardest decision he had ever made, to abandon the search and ride for help. First, he rode to the Kiällberg's, requesting their assistance. Erik and Kerstin responded without hesitation and rode hard for the Raderman farm. The next stop was Emanuel's farm. Again, there was no hesitation as Emanuel loaded up all his children in the wagon and whipped his horse into a gallop.

It was getting late in the day. Dusk at this time of the year came early. When they got back to the Raderman farm, Olof asked Emanuel if his son could ride to get Tobias. Emanuel agreed and sent Olaus to fetch Tobias. Olaus rode quickly to Tobias's croft and was hollering from 20 yards out.

"What happened, Olaus!" Tobias asked, stepping out onto his porch and hooking his suspenders back onto his shoulders.

"My cousin, Kajsa, she is missing!" Olaus shouted as he reined his horse into a skidding stop in front of Tobias. "We need help searching for her!"

"Ja, okay," Tobias said, running to the barn for his horse. After quickly saddling the horse, he charged out of the barn, not waiting for Olaus, who kicked his horse into a gallop. As they rode, Tobias noticed the first few snowflakes fall. Cursing under his breath, he knew any amount of snow would hamper the search. When they arrived at the Raderman farm, Erik had taken charge. Tobias could see the military training in Erik, Emanuel and Olof. Theirs was a more orderly approach while Katarina and Kerstin's were more frantic. Stina was tasked with looking after Barbro, Margareta, Little Emanuel and Jonas. She also kept, without being told, food and drink on the table for the searchers. There was no doubt that they would search throughout the night, if necessary.

The snow continued to fall throughout the night, the temperature below freezing. By the time the sun rose low over the horizon, the searchers were exhausted and hope of finding Kajsa alive began to fade. Olof and Katarina lost only one child before, baby Magdalena. The thought of losing Kajsa at ten years old was beyond heart-wrenching for them.

"Toby, do you think your mother's dogs could find Kajsa?" Emanuel asked him quietly as they stood in the Raderman yard.

"I don't know, Manni," Tobias answered. "She is at the winter pasture in Norge; it is two hundred and forty miles away."

"We will need to find Kajsa, no matter how long it takes," Emanuel said. His meaning was clear to Tobias.

They went to the barn, saddled Tobias's horse and put a bridle on Emanuel's horse. Tobias would ride hard, switching between horses as he went, to spell them.

"Where are you going, Toby?" Olof asked when Tobias led the horses out of the barn.

"I am going to get my mother and the dogs to help with the search."

"I don't want ..." Olof began to object, then nodding, "Tack, Toby!"

Tobias rode out of the yard at a canter. He knew he had to pace himself if the horses were to make the long journey. It took him three days of steady riding, stopping twice for six-hour breaks for rest and nourishment. The first stop was along the road with a creek on one side and a high cliff on the other. Tobias caught and cooked a fish over his campfire. After eating, he leaned back against a tree and pulled his pipe out of his shirt pocket. He dug around and found his tobacco pouch. He had purchased the pipe and tobacco in Umeå, assured they were of the highest quality, imported from Denmark. His first attempt at smoking resulted in dizziness and a coughing fit that also felt like it burned inside his ears. His second attempt resulted in vomiting. After his third attempt, he was hooked. He liked the smell of the sweet tobacco and pictured himself as a well-traveled, wise man when smoking. While puffing on his pipe, he thought he heard a muffled scream.

Suddenly alert, he stood up and looked around, straining to hear. He could see no sign of anyone and the horses didn't seem concerned. Sounds like an owl caught a rabbit; they scream like a little girl when attacked, he thought. He would try to get a few hours of sleep before continuing on his journey. He had been climbing higher in elevation all day and the night promised to be cold. He was glad he had stopped at his farm to get his bearskin blanket.

Chapter 9
Captive

Kajsa sat huddled as far back from the crazy man as she could, utterly terrified. They were in a cave in the side of a mountain. She didn't remember how she got here, waking up with a severe headache and blood-encrusted hair. There was no fire and a rancid piece of raw meat remained untouched in front of her. Because she did not know what animal, or person, the meat came from, she refused to eat it. The crazy man with the dirty face and greasy, wild hair sat across from her, tearing at a chunk of raw meat, ripping it from the bone and chewing loudly.

Suddenly, she caught the scent of wood smoke and an underlying smell, possibly fish cooking? She glanced at the crazy man and tried to work up the courage to scream. After a while, she gave up on that idea, at least until she smelled the pipe smoke. It was the most pleasant aroma she ever experienced, then the crazy man's repugnant body odor washed over her and she let loose a piercing scream. The crazy man leaped across the space between them and covered her mouth with a greasy hand, and her body with his. Her breath was knocked out of her and she frantically started beating at his sides.

"Quiet or I will slit your throat!" His breath smelled like rotten meat as he breathed into her face. She fought back the rising bile in her throat. It was the first words he uttered since he snatched her. The words were in a strange language, but were similar to Swedish so she understood the meaning and steeled herself to be still. After he lifted himself off her, she scurried back against the cave's wall and huddled there the rest of the night. Dánel didn't leave the cave that night, sitting across from her, staring at her. Toward morning, he fell asleep, but Kajsa was too terrified to try escape, even when she heard the sound of distant hooves.

It was now three days since Kajsa had anything to eat. She was able to drink from a drip in the stone wall, carbonate water that she found refreshing. The raw meat he had tossed at her lay rotting on the floor covered with flies. Dánel suddenly jerked awake, startling her.

"I need a fire!" she yelled at him. He stared at her, grunted, farted, got up and left the cave. She heard some noises outside and then it started to get dark. He's locking me inside the cave! Panicked, she ran to the mouth of the cave, seeing a large tree trunk blocking the small cave's opening. Pushing on it, she found it immovable, wedged from the outside. She went back and used a stick to skewer the rotting meat and carried it back to the cave's mouth. She pushed it out a gap between the tree and the cave's opening. Even so, the smell of rotten meat and the stench of the wild man lingered in the cave. With the cave cast into darkness, Kajsa sat against the rear wall, her forehead resting on her knees and hands clasped in front of her shins. She kept repeating a mantra in her head, I am here, Pappa. Come and get me!

Three hours later, she heard the tree trunk being dragged away from the cave mouth. Not knowing what to expect, Kajsa scrabbled back as far as she could against the cave's wall. The wild man came in. He wasn't that tall, but still had to crouch a little as he walked into the cave. Stopping in front of Kajsa, he tossed a dead rabbit, its neck broken, at her feet and dropped a tin can with a candle on top. He then turned and left the cave.

Kajsa picked up the tin and noticed it was a container with a candle holder on top. The candle was burned down, but still had a few inches left. Lifting the top off, she looked inside the tin. Inside was a steel and flint. What am I supposed to do with this? Just as she thought that, the wild man came back in and dumped some firewood, kindling and moss in front of her, then left again. She hoped that whosever's farm he stole the tin from saw him and reported it. She could see the snow on the ground outside and thought his tracks would be easy enough to follow.

Okay, let's see if I can get a fire going!

Kajsa had never watched her parents light a fire, just saw them adding wood to embers in the mornings and blowing on them until the fire caught. She stacked up some wood and then took the flint and steel. She held one in each hand, looking at them with a confused look. Hmm, how would this work? she thought with her tongue sticking out the side of her mouth. Shaking the flint didn't do anything. Next, she started banging them together with no effect. Frustrated, she set them aside and went about the task of cleaning and gutting the rabbit. Among the wood was a green branch which she skewered the rabbit with. Finished, she sat back and looked at the pile of firewood, willing it to burst into flames. Dammit! she thought, setting the rabbit aside and curling up on her pallet, falling asleep shortly afterward.

Kajsa awoke to the sound of wood crackling, heat emanating off the fire and the wild man sitting on the other side of the fire staring at her. She scurried forward and held the rabbit over the fire to cook. Her stomach growled loudly at the smell of the meat cooking, saliva forming in her mouth in anticipation of a meal. Too bad she didn't have a cup for water.

"I want a cup, for water," she croaked.

Grunting, the wild man got up and left the cave. She could hear him dragging the tree stump back into place. It wasn't long before the fire guttered and smoke began to fill the cave. Coughing, Kajsa had no choice but to extinguish the fire. She scattered the burning logs on the stone floor, but the smoke kept filling the room. She went to the cave's entrance and put her face near an opening between the stump and the cave's wall. Breathing deeply of the fresh air, she thought, Stupid man! Looking back into the semi-darkness of the cave to see if it was clear of smoke yet, she noticed tendrils of smoke drifting slowly toward one corner. After breathing in the cold, fresh air from the opening, she crawled on her hands and knees, following the smoke's path.

She hadn't noticed the floor to ceiling outcropping of stone that was overlapping the rear wall of the cave before; it blended so well. The smoke was being drawn around the edge of the outcropping. The darkness was almost complete here, so she felt with her hands the void between the outcropping and wall of the cave. It wasn't much, maybe eight inches, but she did feel a slight drawing of the air going past her hand and out through the void.

Her stomach growled again so she crawled back to get her rabbit. It was only half-cooked, but she was too hungry to care and began ripping off chunks of meat and chewing hungrily. She was leaning back against the cave's wall, sucking the last morsel of meat and marrow from a leg bone when she heard the trunk being moved. The wild man came in and looked at the fire, annoyed and then tossed a tin cup at her feet. She looked at him and said, "You blocked the air into the cave and almost smoked me to death!" Looking back at her, he turned and took a step toward her. She shrunk back, terrified. Seeing this, Dánel grunted and went to lie down by the cave's mouth. Soon, he was snoring, farting and grunting in his sleep. Shuddering, Kajsa thought, I will never get married if all men do that when they sleep!

She crept toward him, judging the opening above his body at the cave's entrance to be about three feet. Could she step over, crouched and get outside without waking him? What if I leap over him in a dive, land on the outside and roll in a crouch, silent as a cat! she thought. Maybe a running start is needed. She walked back a few feet, took a deep breath and ran toward the entrance. She timed her leap perfectly, soaring through the air gracefully above the wild man, and then, cracking her head on the stone opening.

Dánel woke with a start and looked down at the unconscious girl lying on his legs. Rolling her over and into the cave, he muttered, 'Stupid girl!' and went back to sleep. Two hours later, Kajsa woke with a splitting headache. She groaned and gingerly put her hand on her head, feeling the crusted blood. It took a few minutes, but the events leading up to cracking her head on the rock above the cave's opening began to emerge. Slowly turning her head to look behind her, she was horrified to learn she was cradled in the wild man's midsection. Glancing up at his face, she saw that his eyes were open and looking at her. Stifling a scream, she rolled over and scrabbled on her hands and knees to her spot on the other side of the fire pit. Collapsing on her side, she was temporarily blinded by bright lights with sharper points of light at the periphery of her vision. Lying still, breathing heavily, she could feel the lights and pounding pain in her head slowly subside. She could hear his bellowing laughter, which turned almost maniacal, frightening her even more.

That was not good, as her head stabbed with pain with every beat of her heart. He finally stopped laughing, stood in a crouch and waddled out of the cave. For good measure, he let out a thundering blast of gas at the cave's mouth, causing more maniacal laughter. She heard him dragging the tree stump back in front of the opening, dimming the light in the cave. She moved close to the opening, gagging on the smell of his lingering gas and body odor until she breathed in fresh air from the gap above the tree trunk. The air in the cave had become fetid from human waste. She had no other option but to defecate and urinate in a corner of the cave, tearing strips off her dress to clean herself. Not the corner where the smoke vented out, the corner opposite. She would have to change that by moving her waste near the opening so the smell would be drawn out.

Okay, I need to plan my escape better next time. For the rest of the day, she ran different scenarios through her head. Going back to the natural vent, she tested the fit and wedged herself between the gap. She felt a surge of claustrophobic panic when she became stuck between the sides of the opening. Calming herself, she reached out with her hand and felt the opening widen past this pinch point. She also felt a divot in the rock wall that she was able to push on. Sucking in her breath, she pushed hard and slid back out of the gap. Relief flooded through her as she sat there, trying to see into the void. She decided to wait until she had another fire going and the crazy man was sleeping before investing further. Her plan was to set a branch halfway into the fire and then use it as a torch to see into the void. She prayed that it widened into another cave with an opening she could escape out of undetected.

Sitting back behind her fire pit, she once again repeated her silent mantra, I am here, Pappa. Come and get me!

Chapter 10
Winter Pasture

"Toby!" Lovisa said with alarm when Tobias rode into camp looking haggard, with two exhausted horses, "What is it?"

"Hej, Mamma," Tobias said. "Olof's barn, Kajsa, is missing."

"Oh, no! What can I do?"

"Could you come with your dogs to help the search?"

"Of, course!" Lovisa said, "They are not my dogs, but I will ask Válde."

"Tack, Mamma.

"Go get some rest in my lavvu; Dárjá will see to your horses."

* * * *

When Tobias woke, he heard voices outside his mother's lavvu. He didn't realize how tired he was, or it could have been the familiarity of a lavvu that was conducive to his restive sleep. He did miss this; it was better than staying in a log cabin and sleeping on a pole bed. But he did have his bearskin for his cabin bed. He walked out of the lavvu and was met by a group of Sámi.

"Hej, Toby," greeted Válde.

"Hej."

If Válde was offended by not being addressed by his name or title, he did not show it.

With Válde stood Lovisa, Nikko, Jan and the two karelian bear dogs, Jager and Raul.

"Nikko and Jan will come with us, and the dogs," Lovisa said. "We saddled you one of our horses. Yours will rest here until we come back."

"Tack, Mamma," Tobias said. "Let's go."

"Do you have anything of Kajsa's for the dogs to get her scent?"

"Nej, Mamma. Sorry, I wasn't thinking."

"Okay, we will ride to Olof's and start from there."

Lovisa passed him some dried meat and a canteen. He would eat on horseback; time was of the essence. They trotted out of the encampment, taking the trail that would lead them to Hössjö. The dogs ran ahead as they usually did, thinking they were hunting wolves or bears.

Late in the third day, Lovisa called a halt as they were galloping down the trail.

"What is it, Lovisa?" Nikko asked.

"Do you smell that?" Lovisa asked. "Smoke?"

They all came to a stop, sniffing the air. Jager and Raul stopped in the trail ahead of them, looking back impatiently. So far, they caught no whiff of predator scent, still thinking that was their purpose on this outing.

"I don't smell anything," Jan said.

"Nor I," Nikko agreed.

They did not see the snow chunks behind them, falling from the cliffs above the trail.

"Okay, let's go," Lovisa said, frowning, as she kicked her horse into a gallop.

Early on the fourth day, they rode into Olof's yard, and were met by Olof aiming his musket at Jager and Raul.

"Don't shoot, Olof!" Tobias called, "Those are our dogs."

"Did you find Kajsa?" Lovisa asked.

"Nej, no sign," Olof answered, lifting his musket. He looked haggard from worry and lack of sleep.

"Could I have a piece of her clothing, Olof?" Lovisa asked. "For the dogs to get her scent."

"Ja, Katarina will get it for you," Olof said. "And Lovisa?"

"Ja."

"Tack!" Olof said and then went into the cabin. Lovisa watched him go, emotions running through her. After all these years of bitter feelings between them, mostly Olof's, it took a daughter's disappearance to mend their friendship. Katarina came out of the cabin carrying an 'undertröja' [undershirt].

"This is Kajsa's," Katarina said. "Please find my daughter, Lovisa."

"I will try," Lovisa said, taking the garment and handing it to Nikko.

"Take the dogs out of the fence line. Kajsa's scent will be all over the yard."

Nikko took the garment and led the dogs outside the farmyard. He held the undershirt to each dog's nose, letting them get the scent. They began circling the ground, trying to find a scent trail. Nikko led them around the perimeter of the yard, the dogs sniffing and snuffling as they went. Nikko stopped them and held the undershirt under their noses once more before letting them continue. All of a sudden, the dogs stopped, looked north and then bolted into the bush, baying as they went.

"They found her trail!" Tobias called and they charged toward the bush. Once again, the trail was where no horse could easily go. Tobias and Lovisa jumped off their horses and ran after the dogs. There was no need to tell Nikko and Jan what to do.

They gathered Lovisa and Tobias's horse's reins and led them along a trail, roughly in the same direction the dog's baying was leading them. Olof came running behind Lovisa and Tobias, but he was having trouble keeping up with them. He was, after all, forty-seven years old and a veteran of the grueling Pomeranian War. He was not as agile as he once was and he was exhausted from the last several days searching for his daughter. He couldn't remember the last time he slept, certainly not since Kajsa's disappearance.

Tobias ran in the lead. He didn't slow to wait for his mother, knowing she would catch up. He did notice the dogs were leading them in the general direction of the trail to the Sámi winter pasture. The difference being, they were moving upward into the mountainous terrain the trail bordered. Glancing back, he could see his mother climbing the hill behind him, about 50 yards back. He could not see Olof, but he could hear him plowing through the bush. The dogs ahead were baying excitedly and he knew they were closing in on where Kajsa was. He wished over and over in his mind that they would find her alive.

Chapter 11
Kajsa

Kajsa used the time when the wild man was gone to figure out how to use the flint. Quite by accident, she discovered that if struck at an angle with the steel, the flint would produce sparks. *Okay, now I need something for the sparks to ignite.* She looked around and spotted the dry grass under some of the wood the wild man dumped on the cave's floor. After several attempts, the grass caught the sparks and started to smolder only to go out. Maybe it was a memory of her father building a fire, or instinct, when she started blowing gently on the smoldering grass. The grass caught fire, but she had no kindling at hand to keep the fire going.

She gathered small sticks to use as kindling and stacked them like lavvu poles. But she was out of grass now. Frustrated, she sat back and waited for the wild man to return. Suddenly, she felt terrified when she considered the possibility that he wasn't going to return. Locked in the cave, she would die of starvation! As panic set in, she sorted through the firewood for a branch long enough to use as a pry to move the tree stump blocking the cave's opening. Taking the longest piece, she wedged it in a gap under the stump. She realized she needed something under her stick to be able to pry upward and out. Going back to the firewood pile, she selected a few logs and took them back to the stump. Placing one under her branch, she pushed down on it and felt the stump move! Exhilarated, she adjusted the log underneath her branch and tried again. This time she put all her weight on the branch; her feet left the floor as she balanced and bounced on the log. The stump lifted and began to roll outward, away from the cave's opening. Grinning and bouncing on her branch, she felt freedom within her grasp when her branch broke. Down she went to the stone floor, scraping her midsection on the jagged end of the wood. The stump rolled back into place. The scrapes stung fiercely as she lay sobbing on the floor. It was the first time she had allowed herself to cry during her ordeal.

The stump began to move and then was dragged out of the opening. Dánel, bent over, waddled into the cave, stopping to look down at the broken log. He walked over to where Kajsa lay, clutching her belly. He could see the blood seeping through her fingers. Shaking his head, he tossed another rabbit at her feet. Kajsa was surprised when she felt glad that he had returned.

"I need more dry grass," she muttered.

"Eh?"

"I need more dry grass!" she screamed, startling him enough that he took a few steps back. Emboldened, she cried, "Now!"

Muttering under his breath, Dánel walked out of the cave. She sat up and lifted the looped strings from the buttons of her ripped shirt so she could inspect the scraps. The bleeding seemed to have stopped, leaving long streaks of raw scrapes. Closing her shirt, she turned to the task of cleaning the rabbit. She tore and removed the rabbit's thin skin and took it over to cover her feces pile and then scooped up the waste in the skin and carried it over near the vent. The wild man walked back in and tossed some dry grass by her kindling pile. He went back to the opening and sat beside it with his back to the rock wall. He seemed content to sit and watch her.

Kajsa took the grass and pushed it under the tepee of kindling. Taking the flint and steel, she began striking near the grass. Sparks began to fly, some catching in the grass. She bent over and gently blew on the smoldering grass until it burst into flames, the kindling soon catching fire. She added larger pieces of wood as the kindling burned until she had a good fire going. She took the green willow and skewered the rabbit carcass and wedged it under a rock so that it hovered over the fire. Kajsa sat back, pleased with herself, glancing proudly over at the wild man. He grunted and walked out of the cave. She felt disappointed when he didn't seem impressed by her newly learned skills. Then panic set in again as she thought he would plug the cave's opening. But he didn't. She crept over to the opening and peered around the corner. He stuck his face in front of her face and yelled, "BOO!" The rotten breath hit her full face as he laughed hysterically.

"Jäkel [Devil]!" Kajsa cried, fighting down her bile. The curse only heightened the wild man's maniacal laughter. Breathing deeply, Kajsa's stomach settled, then growled at the smell of cooking meat. She went back to the fire and turned the rabbit. She picked up the tin cup she left below the water drip from a crack in the stone wall. It was full and she gulped half of it down, smacking her lips and sighing, "Aah."

She ate the entire rabbit, sucking the marrow out of the bones for good measure. I'll not leave anything for that jäkel. Drinking the last of her water, she placed the cup back below the drip. Her scrapes had scabbed over and had stopped stinging. She crept carefully to the mouth of the cave, seeing the man sitting with his back against a tree about 10 feet away. Running by him wouldn't work; he would hear her feet on the snow and trip or grab her as she went past. She wasn't sure she could outrun him even if she did get by him.

She crept back to the fire and picked up the piece of wood that she set partially into the fire. To her relief, the piece of wood continued to burn after she removed it from the flames. Glancing back to the cave's mouth, she eased her way over to the hidden void in the back of the cave. Holding the torch in front of her, she peered into the void, panicking when her torch guttered. Breathing a sigh of relief, the torch flamed again, even larger than before. Looking into the void, her heart dropped when she saw that it did not go very far. So where was the air being sucked out to? Glancing up, she saw a wisp of her torch's smoke rise into the ceiling.

Is that a sliver of daylight? She pushed herself between the opening, careful not to get stuck again, and looked up. She could see a void above the small space, like a chimney.

Could I climb up there? Does it lead outside or taper to nothing? She eased back out of the void's opening and made her way back to her fire. She needed to think about the risks of an attempted escape through the chimney. If she got stuck in the chimney, she would surely starve to death, or even freeze! But what was the alternative — stay at the mercy of a wild man, who, at any time, could tire of her and kill her, or disappear and leave her trapped? She decided to wait until he left in the morning; those were the times he was gone the longest, and attempt her escape up the chimney.

Chapter 12
Jager and Raul

Tobias stopped to catch his breath, trying to hear over his ragged breathing. The dog's baying had increased and had an excited, or terrified, quality. They must be close, he thought. Lovisa was making her way up to his position.

"You hear that?" Tobias called.

Gasping for breath, Lovisa could only nod. She came up to where Tobias was leaning against a tree. His breathing had slowed to a comfortable level, but he waited for his mother to catch her breath. They were standing there when they heard one of the dogs yelp. The other had quit baying.

"Come on!" Lovisa cried, "One of them is hurt!" Not waiting for Tobias, Lovisa charged headlong in the direction they last heard the dogs. She stopped when she heard the next yelp. "Oh, no!" she said softly, "not both of them!"

They came to a stream and could see where the dogs had run along one side of the bank.

"Mamma!" Tobias cried, "Wait for me!"

Lovisa was about to bolt after the dogs but looked back at Tobias.

He stopped beside her, gasping for breath, and then pulled his pistol from his belt.

"What do you have?" he asked.

She lifted a hatchet from its loop at her waist and then produced a fearsome-looking knife.

"Okay, let's go!" Tobias said, and they ran along the bank. They had to be careful. The snow had melted some and it made the muddy bank greasy. After a few minutes, they stopped short when they saw Jager crawling toward them. He was covered in blood and his back legs didn't seem to be working. Lovisa ran to him and knelt in front of him. The dog whimpered and licked her hand with a bloody mouth before collapsing onto its side. Lovisa checked his body for injuries. There was a lot of blood, but she didn't think any of it was his. "What happened to you, Jager?" she whispered to the dog. Jager rolled his eyes to look at her and Lovisa noticed his tail remained still. Torn by what to do, she waved Tobias on, staying with Jager. She couldn't leave the faithful dog to die alone in the cold.

Tobias glanced down briefly at the dog before leaping over him and continuing along the creek bank. Lovisa took off her coat and laid it over Jager. She attempted to lay her coat on the cold ground and roll him over onto it, but he yelped and nipped at her when she tried to roll him. "I am sorry, Jager!" she cried, at a loss as to what to do. So, she sat beside him and set Jager's head on her lap. Petting the side of his face and head, she sang a Sámi lullaby to calm him.

After what seemed like an eternity, but was actually only fifteen minutes, Tobias came walking back.

"Raul is dead. His throat was ripped open," Tobias said.

"Oh! Was it a bear or wolves?"

"Neither. This was a man, a wild man," Tobias said. "From the amount of blood on the ground, they must have torn him up pretty bad before he managed to stab and cut Raul's neck. I found the knife; I think Jager must have bitten into Pappa's, ahh, I mean the man's wrist for him to drop it." Lovisa swung her head around, glaring at him, then softening as she said quietly, "We don't know for sure it is Dánel."

"Ja, of course, Mamma. Sorry."

They heard Olof grunting and blowing as he neared them.

Lovisa stood and looked toward where Jager had come from. She couldn't see anything, other than the dog's drag marks.

Olof was obviously struggling. He reached them and put a hand on a tree to steady himself. Lovisa and Tobias waited patiently while he caught his breath. He was looking down at Jager with a puzzled look as his breathing gradually slowed.

"What happened?" he gasped.

"The dogs caught up with the killer," Tobias stated.

"He killed my dog and may have crippled this one!" Lovisa said forcefully. She then realized it wasn't Olof's fault and quickly said, "Sorry, Olof, these dogs mean a lot to me."

"Ja, and my daughter means a lot to me!" Olof said, "What are you waiting for?"

"It will be dark soon. We will begin again in the morning," Lovisa said.

"What?" Olof bellowed, "I'll not give up until I find her!"

"Do what you want, Olof," Lovisa said quietly. "Tobias and I are going to take Jager back to his croft and then we will start again in the morning."

"Olof, you are going to wander around in the dark, maybe destroying any sign of them and you would be an easy target for him," Tobias said.

"What did you say to me, you little skit?" Olof bellowed, taking on an aggressive stance. Lovisa stood and said, "Go ahead. We will bring your body back tomorrow."

She turned to Tobias and said, "We need to make a stretcher

for Jager."

Olof pushed his way past them and started down the path along the creek. He didn't make it too far before slipping on the mud and sliding into the ice-cold creek. "Förbaske [Dammit]!" he bellowed. He tried crawling out of the creek, but couldn't find anything to grab. Tobias walked over and held out his hand. Olof stared at him, then reached up and grabbed his hand. Tobias braced his feet and pulled Olof out of the creek. He began shivering immediately. Tobias then took the hatchet Lovisa was holding out to him and walked over to chop some saplings for the stretcher. Olof was shivering uncontrollably now, teeth clacking.

"Take off your clothes, Olof," Lovisa said. "Tobias, give him your coat until he warms up." She got up and began collecting dead, dry wood wherever she could. By the time she got a fire going, Olof's exposed legs and feet were blue. Tobias's coat helped, but he continued to shiver as he hopped from foot to foot.

Tobias and Lovisa were working on the stretcher, casting occasional glances at Olof, both thinking the same thing — Will we have to make another stretcher? Olof's clothes were hung above the fire after Lovisa wrung out as much water as she could. Huge clouds of steam rose, droplets of water hissing in the fire.

Lovisa tore a strip of cloth from the bottom of her shirt and tied it around Jager's mouth.

"He may try to bite when we move him onto the stretcher," Lovisa said. "Let's try to turn him over. I want to make sure he's not bleeding."

They placed the stretcher beside Jager and moved to his front. Tobias held his rear paw and slid his hand underneath the dog. Jager whined, but Lovisa was petting his head and talking softly to him.

"Now, easy," she said as she rolled Jager over. The dog yelped repeatedly behind the clothed tied around his mouth. "I'm sorry, Jager," Lovisa said over and over. Tears were flowing freely now and she put her forehead to the side of Jager's face. He gradually calmed and lay still. At first, they thought of dragging the stretcher behind them but quickly dismissed that thought. The rough terrain would be excruciating for the dog. They picked up an end each and carried Jager as gently as they could.

"Take him to my croft; it is closer," Olof said from behind them as he began putting on his still-damp clothes. He still shivered, but it was no longer an uncontrollable shaking.

Chapter 13
Kajsa

Kajsa was looking through a gap between the tree stump and the cave opening. Jäkel, as she began to think of him, had not yet returned. He was always back before dark, usually to throw some dead animal or rodent at her to cook. She thought she could hear wolves fighting in the distance, but couldn't be sure. Kajsa was worried, not about him, at least she didn't think so, but about being trapped in this cave if he didn't return. The cave was now in total darkness, so she crawled to her spot and lay down on the cold stone floor. She had spread what little grass and moss she had for a bed, but it was woefully inadequate. Shivering, she curled up in a ball and tried to sleep.

Sometime during the night, she was awakened by a sniffing and scratching noise coming from outside the cave. Heart hammering, she looked toward the cave opening, but it was too dark to see anything. She strained her ears to hear. After a while, she decided she had been dreaming and curled up again. The cold was seeping into her bones so she stood and did some exercises, thinking she would stop before she broke a sweat. That would not be good. She was running in place, panting when she stopped dead and listened intently. Was that an animal trying to get in? Her imagination began to run wild, thinking. Maybe it's a forest troll angry because I was in his cave? And skat in his cave too! Forest trolls were a part of Swedish folklore. Tales of children being captured by trolls usually ended with the child outsmarting the troll. Is Jäkel actually a troll?

She crawled back to her spot, grabbing a stick from the fire pile on the way. She sat against the back wall, then scooted forward because the stone was so cold. With her knees up in front of her and her stick at the ready, she settled in to wait for morning. At some point, she drifted off and lay down. Opening her eyes, she could see daylight coming in the gaps in the tree stump. She looked around her cave and was relieved not to see Jäkel. Then terror began to set in; he had not come back! After her failed attempt to pry the tree trunk out of the way, Jäkel made sure there were no long logs in the cave. Shivering, she scrabbled over to the opening and looked through a gap. She felt warm air through the gap and noticed the snow had all but melted. Water dripped from somewhere above the cave's mouth. Her stomach rumbled, reminding her it had been over a day since she had last eaten.

Kajsa went back to her spot to wait for Jäkel to come back and pull the tree stump away from the opening so she could at least have a fire. She opened her eyes and was stunned to see the ray of sunlight coming through the gap was at a longer angle. She did not remember closing her eyes, but she had fallen asleep again. She got up and crept to the opening and looked out. There was no sign of Jäkel. Is he dead? she thought, alarmed at the prospect. She sat by the tree stump looking out, occasionally yelling, "Jäkel!" But she was met with silence.

The sun was almost completely down when Kajsa made up her mind that the next morning, she was going to squeeze through the gap between the back wall and the stone slab. She planned to climb up through the chimney. She didn't know if there was enough room or if she could even climb it. But she reasoned, it was either try or starve to death sitting here.

She didn't sleep much that night, if at all. Her stomach was cramping from hunger and the cold was relentless. Finally, Kajsa saw some light coming through the gaps in the opening. She checked to see if Jäkel had been back. He hadn't. All the snow was gone, water still dripped off the mountain and birds were singing in the trees. She was more determined than ever to get out of this crypt. She went to the gap between the slab and back wall and, before she could change her mind, pushed herself into the crevice.

As expected, Kajsa's upper torso became wedged at the narrowest part of the crevice. Fighting down her panic, she calmed herself, inhaled and tried to wiggle through. She wasn't sure, but she thought she was inching deeper into the fissure. Finally, she felt an easing of pressure on her chest. And then she was through, plopping onto the floor of the cavity. Whew! Good thing I don't have my teats yet.

Looking up the chimney, she could see blue sky about 20 feet up. It looked like there was enough room for her to climb up there, but how? The ceiling was just above her head. She could see little cavities and protruding rock that she could use as hand and footholds. From years of running barefoot, Kajsa knew she would have a better grip with bare feet instead of shoes. She tried throwing them up the chimney, but they didn't go very far before bouncing off the sides of the chimney and falling back down. After a few attempts, she gave up and went to the crevice and tossed them back into the cave. She never thought of why she did that. It just seemed the right thing to do.

Swinging her arms to loosen her muscles, she crouched down and leaped up into the chimney. Her hands caught a protruding rock but slipped off and she landed on the floor. The drop was only a few feet. Looking up, Kajsa realized she needed to plan her moves if she was going to make it up the chimney. Okay, jump. Grab there with my right hand, there with my left. Pull up and grab there with my right. Pull up and grab there with my left, there with my right. Wedge my right foot there and my left foot there, then rest. She repeated the scenario several times before her next attempt. After taking several breaths and drying her hands on her shirt, she leaped up, grabbing the same protruding rock with one hand and another on the other side with her left. Swinging and kicking her feet, to what end she wasn't sure, but it seemed to help.

Pulling herself up, muscles in her arms straining, she let go with her right hand and grabbed the next handhold. Keeping her momentum, she kept pulling herself up, grabbing the next handhold. Finally, her feet caught purchase and she was able to put most of her weight on her feet and legs, relaxing her arms.

Looking down, Kajsa thought, that would hurt. She wasn't necessarily afraid of heights when playing in barn lofts with her sisters and cousins, but she knew she would perish here if she fell. With a heightened sense of urgency, she looked up and planned her next set of hand and footholds. This one was easier than the first, beginning with footholds; there was no need for strenuous arm strain. Up she went like a monkey, not that she had ever seen or heard of a monkey. She was tempted to continue, but erred on the side of safety. She looked up and could feel the air flowing by her from the cave up and out the chimney. One more climb and she would be at the top. After planning the next set of hand and footholds, envisioning her climb, she pushed up, and slipped.

She fell two feet, banging a knee on the rock wall, before her feet caught purchase on the sides of the chimney. Her perch was tenuous at best, so she quickly secured handholds. Sobbing in relief, she rested as long as she dared, her feet threatening to slip off the little pieces of stone jutting out. After her heart slowed and she tested her knee by putting all her weight on that leg, she determined it was bruised but not damaged. Kajsa decided to go for broke and scale the remainder of the chimney in one quick climb. Up she went, not hesitating as she gabbed whatever handhold she could, running her feet up the sides, using what grip her bare soles allowed on the stone. Finally grabbing the top rim, she pulled herself up and out, onto a small shelf. Lying on her back, not daring to look at how high this shelf was, fearing the worst. Seeing the top of a spruce tree to her left, she rolled over and looked down. The chimney sloped steeply down from 10 feet high to a solid rock floor. "Skit!" she screamed.

On her hands and knees, she looked around the lip of her chimney. The mountain climbed on the other side. Looking up, she quickly dismissed the route as unclimbable, at least in her condition, and without any climbing aids. She looked around trying to orient herself. Kajsa remembered looking west to the mountains from her home on many occasions, so she looked to the lowlands. That was the direction she must go; she would find a road and follow it.

An eagle soared near her, his head turning and his beady eyes sizing her up as a possible meal. "Fek off, ya filthy buzzard!" she cried. Kajsa had heard her father curse when he was changing a wagon wheel and it was the first time that she had repeated it out loud. She grinned to herself, standing and shouting at the receding eagle, "Fek off, fek off, fek off!" she shouted and then ran a couple of steps across the chimney and leaped through the air toward the spruce tree. She hit the tree hard, boughs and branches tearing at her skin before slamming into the trunk, knocking the wind out of her. Scraped and bleeding, Kajsa hung on tightly until she got her breath back and the tree stopped swaying. She climbed down the tree to solid ground easily enough. Standing at the bottom, she felt immense relief and pride at her achievement.

She took stock of her injuries, mostly cuts and scrapes that stung. Her knee ached but didn't seem to be seriously damaged. Which way? she wondered. She realized she was on a shelf, so she walked to the edge and looked down. Through the leafless poplar trees, she could just make out patches of what appeared to be packed earth, a trail! Now, how to get down there safely? Kajsa began walking along the edge of the shelf watching for a gentle slope down when she rounded a corner and was surprised to see the entrance to her cave. Of course, her cave would be somewhere near, but as she came around the bend, she saw Jäkel lying to the side of the cave's opening. Shockwaves of fear coursed through her body. Her fear slowly dissipated and was replaced by concern. She could see that he wasn't moving and his pants appeared to be covered with blood. Was he dead? Could she outrun him now if he wasn't dead but seriously injured? She picked up a dead branch and inched toward him, first poking at his feet, then legs, then his stomach, hard. No response.

Suddenly, Kajsa thought of her shoes lying in the cave. Making up her mind, she decided to see if she could move the tree enough to squeeze back into the cave to get her shoes. She looked at the tree, seeing the wedges Jäkel had braced it with. She pulled those away, always watching Jäkel for any movement as she did. With the braces gone, she was able to roll the tree back, panicking when it looked like it would roll right over Jäkel. She cried out and tried to stop its roll, spotting a brace by her feet. She kicked it under, stopping the tree. That hurt. Why did I do that? The Jäkel is already dead! she thought. Taking a deep breath, she steeled herself for the run back into the cave to get her shoes. With one final look at Jäkel, she bolted into the cave and grabbed one shoe, frantically looking for the other one. She finally spotted it, scooped it up and ran back out of the cave. She was passing where Jäkel was lying when a hand reached out and grabbed her ankle, toppling her forward and down. Panicking, she began kicking at the hand with her free foot, breaking the weak hold easily. Looking at his face, she was shocked to see him looking back at her — was that a pleading look? She scrabbled back and put her shoes on. His head dropped back down and as she stood, she carefully circled Jäkel so she could see the extent of his injuries. It looked like he was set upon by wolves, exposed meat from gory tears ripped out of the back of his thigh, the pants below covered in dried blood. Both his forearms looked torn. And lots of torn clothing. She guessed that the tough hide clothing had probably saved him from further injuries. A wave of dizziness passed through her. She had not eaten in two days and the exertion of her climb to freedom took a lot out of her. Suddenly weary, she sat down with her back to a tree. I will just rest a minute before I leave, she thought.

Kajsa opened her eyes and then bolted upright as she remembered where she was and who was lying 10 feet away from her. Jäkel had indeed moved several feet toward her, but now he lay unconscious. Jumping up, Kajsa moved to put the tree between herself and Jäkel and then reached down to pick up her stick. A wave of dizziness hit her as she straightened up. When that passed, she looked at Jäkel to see if he was still alive. She could see his side lifting slightly with each shallow breath he took. One of his hands lay outstretched toward her and seemed to be clutching a hide pouch.

Curiosity won out over her instinct to run fast and far from this man. Watching his face closely, Kajsa inched toward him with her stick raised in one hand, ready to strike if he made the slightest movement. With her heart pounding, she reached out to the pouch and quickly yanked it out of his hand. Running back to the tree, she once again stood behind it as she watched Jäkel's body for any sign of movement. Looking down at the pouch, she slowly undid the hide cord that tied the opening closed. Peering inside, she saw what appeared to be chunks of thick leather. Reaching and taking one out, she discovered that it was actually dried meat; from what animal, she did not know. Taking a sniff, her stomach rumbled and her mouth began to water. She had smelled and tasted dried reindeer meat before, when her father had come back from trading with the Sámi.

"How long have you been keeping this to yourself, you fekking Jäkel"? she cried before biting into the meat and closing her eyes in pleasure. She managed to eat a large chunk of the dried meat before the stomach cramps began. They hit with such force that she fell to the ground and curled up in a fetal position. I will not throw up this food! she thought as her stomach spasmed.

When the spasms gradually dissipated, Kajsa stood and walked around Jäkel toward the cave's opening. Emboldened, she went into the cave and drank deeply from her cup, placing it back under the drip by habit. She went out and walked away from the cave without looking back. There was a trace of an old trail, barely distinguishable, but it offered a route down to the track she had seen from the shelf. Using saplings for handholds, Kajsa made her way down to the track. She turned right and began her walk home. After walking a hundred yards, Kajsa stopped and looked over her shoulder. Cursing to herself, she turned and began walking back toward the cave. *I should leave him for the vultures!*

Chapter 14
Trondheim

"What is wrong, Pehr?" Gunhild asked. "You have been quiet lately."

"I am restless, Hilda. I have been thinking of taking a trip, preferably not by boat."

Pehr suffered debilitating seasickness whenever he traveled by ship.

"The only place you can go by land is southern Norway, seeing as you can't go through Sweden," Axel said.

They were in the Paulsen's parlor after finishing their evening meal. Axel was smoking his pipe and all three were enjoying their coffee.

"Ja, I know." Pehr sighed.

"After all these years, do you think anyone would recognize you?" Gunhild asked.

"All it takes is one and he has escaped capture twice. You can bet there are some who would like the honor of catching the elusive Pehr Olofsson, master of evasion!" Axel chuckled at his wit. Pehr and Gunhild smiled graciously.

"Oslo is nice this time of year. You can spend some of your shoe fortune there. Do some shopping." Gunhild grinned. "Maybe buy some gifts?"

"I would like to go back to Lübeck, visit my old friends, but that involves a sea voyage."

Pehr had suffered a deep depression in the aftermath of the

Pomeranian War. He had come out of it after moving in with the Paulsens and then resuming his shoemaking trade. Now, even after all his success, Pehr felt himself slipping into a mild depression and it terrified him.

"Well, you will have to weigh the good and the bad of such a voyage," Axel opined, sucking on his pipe for dramatic effect, exhaling the sweet-smelling smoke before he continued. "Seasickness, both ways I'll wager, against visiting your friends from fourteen years past. I will caution that some may not be of this world anymore."

"I had not thought of that. Horst, Karl and Otto were older men when I lived there," Pehr said. "Sophia had married the fishmonger and probably has several little ones by now."

Horst was a stable owner who had befriended Pehr after his escape from Pomerania and Otto was the shoemaker's shop owner and Horst's brother-in-law who had hired Pehr. Karl was a master shoemaker who taught Pehr the trade. Sophia was the granddaughter of the farm couple to whom the Prussians army had commanded the care and confinement of Pehr. In return, the farm couple were granted the use of the prisoner for slave labor. After Pehr regained his memory at the end of the war, he rescued Sophia, then fourteen, from a life of misery with abusive grandparents and their adventures eventually led them to the port town of Lübeck in northern Prussia.

"I shall have to consider it," Pehr said, rising from his seat. "I am going to take a wander down to the tavern. Anyone interested in joining me?"

"Well, if you are going to twist my arm, I guess I will have to. Hilda?"

"Ja, a nice walk will help the digestion."

And so, it was that Pehr was in the tavern when none other than Oscar Hanemman, a crew member of the ship that Pehr traveled from Lübeck to Trondheim on, these fourteen years past, was standing at the bar. Perhaps it was the recent thoughts of ship travel that evoked the memory of the sailor in Pehr's mind. Or, perhaps it was just coincidence, but Pehr thought that his eyes would have normally passed over this man without a second thought.

"I think I know that man!" Pehr said after studying him for several minutes. They were seated at their customary table near the door. "He is a lot older, but I am sure it's the first mate on the ship I sailed on from Lübeck."

"Are you sure, Pehr?" Axel asked. "It has been a long time and you were ill most of the way."

"I was ill all of the way!" Pehr said. "He was kind to me, brought me water after some bad bouts hanging over the rail."

"That is a sign, if it is him!" Gunhild said.

She had lately taken an interest in both palm and tarot reading, convinced she was a bit psychic. Axel saw no harm in it and humored her whenever she wanted to practice her 'gift.' That is, until Gunhild saw in the cards that Axel would meet a beautiful woman. She had leaped up from her seat, called Axel a cheating pig and ran to their bedroom, locking the door behind her. Pehr ran into the parlor to see what the commotion was all about, seeing Axel sitting at the card table with a bewildered look on his face and asked, "What happened?"

"I don't rightly know!" Axel said. "Apparently, I am going to meet a beautiful woman sometime in my future."

"Humph, I wonder if she will read my future?" Pehr asked.

"I would strongly advise against it, Pehr!"

That was several months past and all had been forgiven, Axel and Pehr begging off whenever Gunhild offered a reading. They would tell her life was better with an air of mystery.

Pehr continued to study the man at the bar. "I will go ask him if we have ever met before. I just wish I could remember his name!" Gathering their empty cups, Pehr limped over to the bar. The limp was a lingering reminder of the beating he took when he was robbed. It was not noticeable unless he had been sitting for an extended period, or when he was nervous. He stood beside the man and ordered another round for his table. Glancing over at the man casually, he asked, "You look familiar. Were you ever a first mate on a ship called the 'Catharina'?"

"Now that is going back!" the man replied. "Do I know you, friend?"

"My name is Pehr. I was aboard your ship traveling from Lübeck to here." The man just stared at him.

"I was seasick the entire voyage."

"The shoemaker?"

"Ja, that was me!"

Of course, as is the case when casual acquaintances meet in a tavern, the reaction was as if they were long-lost friends meeting by chance. They grinned broadly at each other, shaking hands vigorously and exchanging over-zealous compliments on each other's lack of aging and overall good looks.

"Come sit with me and my friends. We are over by the door," Pehr offered when their exuberance waned.

"Ja, gladly, let me get another drink first."

"It is on me!" Pehr declared.

"Danke!"

"Go on over and introduce yourself and I will bring the

drinks," Pehr said as a ploy to learn the man's name. He had been racking his brain, trying to remember. Straining to hear over the tavern's din while waiting for the drinks, Pehr could hear Axel introducing himself and his wife but, maddeningly, uproarious laughter erupted from a nearby table just as the man introduced himself. Coming back to the table, trying not to spill any of the four drinks in his hands, Pehr placed the steins on the table and lifting his, he said, "Skål!"

"Skål," came the reply.

"So, tell me, Oscar," Axel said, glancing at Pehr, who smiled with gratitude, "are you still a seaman?"

"Aye, these legs are not meant for dry land!"

"Pehr here was considering a voyage back to Lübeck to visit old friends," Axel said.

"Ja?" Oscar looked dubiously at Pehr. "Are you still afflicted with the seasickness?"

"I would presume so," Pehr replied. "It has been fourteen years so I am not sure."

"It is not something that one overcomes, my friend," Oscar said. "Although I have heard ether drops help somewhat."

"Ether?" Axel exclaimed. "What they use to knock people out for surgery?"

"Ja, but not too much. It is supposed to calm the stomach. You put several drops on a lump of sugar and drop it in ginger tea."

"That is interesting. I could read your cards, Pehr, to see if it will work?" Gunhild said.

"Ahhh, maybe before I leave."

"Ja, that is good. The signs will be stronger," Gunhild said. "I am a bit psychic, Oscar, if you would like me to read your palm?"

Axel and Pehr both looked at Oscar with alarm, causing Oscar to reply, "Ahh, we seamen are a superstitious lot, Gunhild. It is considered bad luck to have our fortunes told before a voyage." It was a spontaneous lie; an ability Oscar had cultivated over many years while drinking in taverns.

"Call me Hilda," Gunhild replied, "and I understand completely. The dark arts are not to be trifled with!"

"Where will your travels take you next, Oscar?" Axel asked.

"Gothenberg. We ship out in two days."

"Do you know of any ships leaving for Lübeck?" Pehr asked.

"Nej, sorry, my friend, but I can ask around and let you know."

They traded stories for several hours, well past their usual quitting time and they were quite inebriated.

Late the next afternoon, Pehr was still feeling the effects of his hangover when Oscar rushed into his shoe store with an exuberance that no man should have after a night of hard drinking.

"Pehr!" he shouted. "I found a ship that will dock in Lübeck! You can get passage, but it leaves in one hour!"

"One hour!" cried Pehr. "I haven't even packed!"

"The next ship going there may be a month away."

"Okay, can you tell the captain I will be there?" Pehr asked. "I will have to go to the bank for some money. I guess I could buy what I need there."

"Ja, ja, but hurry, my friend. They will not wait."

Pehr rushed over to his bank and, given his standing as a successful businessman with substantial funds deposited in the bank, he was hustled over to the bank manager's office without delay. Pehr took out a rather large sum, not sure what the ship's passage would be or his meals, accommodations and clothes for that matter. He walked swiftly out of the bank, alert to any threat. He remembered all too well the last time he was near the docks with a large amount of money.

He made it in time, just as a crewman was about to pull in the boarding ramp. Running across the ramp onto the ship's deck, it crossed Pehr's mind that he had not picked up any ether or ginger root from the apothecary.

Chapter 15
Olof

The walk back to Olof's farm took longer than any of them thought it would. Lovisa and Tobias had to be careful with their footing lest they drop Jager. Olof stumbled along behind them, head down and shivering. They became quite concerned when they stopped to wait for him to catch up. Lovisa asked Olof if he was okay and he mumbled something incoherently with a confused look on his ashen face. Lovisa decided that they needed to build a fire and that Tobias should run ahead to get help. After setting Jager down and helping to collect dry wood, Tobias ran toward Olof's farm. Lovisa cut and laid spruce bows down for Olof to lie on and covered him with her coat. With the fire started, she sat beside Jager and laid her hand on his head. 'Did his tail just twitch?' She stared at Jager's tail, but it did not move. She was sure it had twitched.

Olof lay by the fire fast asleep. She suspected exhaustion had finally caught up to him and she was sure he wasn't eating properly since Kajsa's disappearance. As she watched Olof sleeping, Lovisa thought about her own daughter, Dárjá, and what she would be going through if it was Dárjá who had disappeared. She felt a surge of compassion for Olof as she thought of all the emotions he must have gone through since the disappearance.

In less than an hour, Tobias, Nikko and Jan came running into their camp.

"I met them on the trail." Tobias panted. "They were going up and down the trail listening for the dogs when I ran into them."

"Okay, let's get these two out to the horses," Lovisa said.

Nikko and Jan made a makeshift sling out of Tobias's coat and carried Olof between them. Olof stirred but did not wake up when they lifted him. Lovisa and Tobias followed them with Jager between them on his stretcher. Getting back to the horses, Nikko and Jan laid Olof over the back of one horse and Tobias climbed up behind him. Lovisa mounted her horse and led Nikko and Jan's horses as the two Sámi hunters walked behind, carrying Jager on his stretcher.

It was full dark when Lovisa and Tobias rode into the Raderman farmyard. A glow from candles and lanterns lighted the porch as Katarina came out with Olof's musket at the ready.

"Hej, Katarina, we brought Olof home," Lovisa called.

Katarina dropped the musket, let out a wail and ran toward Olof who was still draped unconscious over Tobias's horse.

"Nej, Katarina!" Lovisa cried, aware of her mistake. "Olof is alive and well. He just collapsed from exhaustion!"

Katarina lifted Olof's head in her hands and didn't stop crying until she confirmed her husband was alive.

"Oh, dear God, you gave me a fright, Lovisa!"

"Ja, I am sorry, Kajsa. I wasn't thinking."

Tobias helped Katarina lift Olof off the horse and carry him into the cabin. They carried him through to their bedroom and laid him on the bed, Katarina removing his still damp clothes and covering him with a mound of bed rolls.

"Hej, the camp!" Nikko called from the yard.

'This is not a camp!' Katarina muttered.

"Is it okay if we bring in my dog, Katarina?" Lovisa asked. "He was attached during the search."

"Of course. Put him by the hearth."

Nikko and Jan laid Jager gingerly down near the hearth and the Raderman girls immediately surrounded him, all wanting to pet him.

"Be careful, min älsklings, he is injured and can't be moved!" Lovisa warned.

"What happened to him?" Anna asked.

"I don't know. We were behind him when someone attacked them. Raul is dead."

"Oh, no!" the three girls all cried at once.

"Can we keep him?" Stina asked.

"I am sorry, Stina," Lovisa responded. "He belongs with the people, the Sámi."

The three girls were sitting around Jager, all petting him gently when Lovisa saw his tail move slightly. Relief flooded through her as she realized Jager might possibly walk again.

"What is his name, Auntie?" Brita asked.

"Jager."

The girls all began to tell Jager how he was such a good boy and his tail thumped once, then again.

"We will go out again before first light, Kajsa," Lovisa said, not being able to hide her weariness.

"That is good, Lovisa. Anna, come and help with the food," Katarina said. "After you have something to eat, I will make a bed for you. The men can sleep in the barn again."

"Tack," came the reply from the men.

Embracing Lovisa, Katarina whispered, "I am grateful to you for bringing my husband home."

Chapter 16
Jäkel

On the way back to the cave, Kajsa gathered dry wood, grumbling the whole time. She had to throw the sticks up the incline, some of them falling short of the shelf and tumbling back down until being stopped by a sapling or other protuberance on the slope. Careful not to slip, Kajsa made her way up the slope, stopping now and then to pick up and throw a piece of firewood.

Jäkel had not moved other than curling into a fetal position. She gave him a wide berth going into the cave, remembering the start he gave her by grabbing her ankle. She had become quite adept at starting a fire with the flint and steel and soon a fire crackled in the cave. Next, she went out and stood looking down at Jäkel, wondering how she was going to get him into the cave. She couldn't leave him; wild animals and other scavengers would come before long.

Kajsa still had the stick arms of a ten-year-old, but she did have the strength of someone accustomed to doing daily farm chores. The cuts and scrapes of the climb of the chimney and the descent of the tree still stung, but her performance had given Kajsa confidence. So, without further hesitation, she took hold of Jäkel under his arms and began tugging at his dead weight. He was immovable. Next, she tried rolling him, which resulted in Jäkel waking, hissing from the pain of his open wound when it touched the ground.

"I'm sorry, Jäkel," Kajsa said. "You have to help me get you into the cave before wolves or bears come to eat you!"

He looked up at her with unnervingly large, pain-filled eyes for several seconds before he nodded. She once again grabbed him under his arms and began tugging. This time he helped her by pushing with the foot of his good leg and one arm while keeping his wounded hamstring away from the ground. After much exertion, they made it fireside where Kajsa positioned him behind the fire, thinking that it would be good if there was a fire between him and any predator entering the cave.

She retrieved the cup of water from the drip and brought it back to him. After drinking the entire cup, Jäkel lay back and immediately fell asleep. Kajsa took the cup back to the drip, intending to make a broth by putting a chunk of dried meat into the enamel cup and boiling it. She decided that she would eat the meat and he could have the broth. She also decided that when all the dried meat was gone, so was she. He would have to fend for himself after that. After all, she owed him nothing.

While waiting for the cup to fill, she decided to stock up on wood and see what could be foraged in the area. Her mother had often taken Kajsa and her sisters into the forest to pick berries and mushrooms along with roots and various plants that she would use for tea or medicinal purposes. Kajsa now wished she had paid more attention when her mother explained what the plants were used for.

Walking down the track, she kept an eye out for edible plants and wildlife. Given the time of year, Kajsa was not optimistic about her chances, but after a half-hour, she spotted some rönnbär [rowan berries]. These edible berries had a sour taste, but she was glad she found them. As she gathered the berries, she thought of her mother reciting an old saying when picking these berries last summer, "De är sura, sa räven om rönnbären," ["They are sour, said the fox about the rowan berries"]. On her way back to the track, she spotted some large cep mushrooms under a spruce tree. Proud of her haul, Kajsa made her way back to the cave.

Jäkel was still asleep when she got back so she went to retrieve her cup. Adding wood to the fire, she drank some water and then placed a piece of dried meat into the cup and put it on the fire. She would boil the berries afterward, not wanting to make the broth sour tasting. While waiting for the water to boil, she cleaned the mushrooms by scraping the spongy undersides with her fingernails and then breaking the mushrooms into chunks. She then speared the mushroom pieces with a green willow and placed them over the fire to roast.

When the water had boiled, she fished the meat out and tossed it hand to hand until it cooled enough to eat. She ate some roasted mushrooms between bites of meat and moaned with satisfaction. The meal could only get better with a dessert of cooked rönnbär, but she had to wait for Jäkel to wake up and drink his broth. She only had the one cup. I wonder where he got the cup, and the flint and steel? she thought. He hadn't been gone the whole day when she asked for and received the cup. Placing the cup of broth near Jäkel, she went out of the cave and walked around the shelf. It was mid-afternoon and she hoped to catch sight of wood smoke from someone's farm. Seeing none, she walked back and around the other way. She realized she could only see a small portion of the surrounding area as the shelf only extended about a hundred feet around the hill. It was too small to be called a mountain, but it was still quite large.

Better go feed Jäkel before the broth gets cold, she thought and went back inside the cave. Jäkel had not stirred so she sat down and shook him. Nothing. "Hmmm." She said, "I am going to enjoy this!" and slapped him hard across the face. "Fek!" she cried, shaking her hand. Jäkel stirred and opened his eyes, staring at her. "About fekking time, you arsel!" she cried. She knelt beside his head, lifting it with one hand and lifting the broth to his mouth with her other.

"I better not get lice from the rat's nest you call hair!" she said.

He grunted and sipped the broth slowly, not trusting her, but he was in no position to refuse. "I will need to clean your wounds if I can find something to carry the water in," she said. "This cup is too small." He mumbled something after she took the cup away from his mouth.

"What?"

"A farm, to the south, about two miles." He breathed, causing her to fight back her rising bile. "Go right on the track and right again when you come to a small creek. It will take you to the farm." He lay back, exhausted, but she raised his head again. "Finish this. I need the cup."

After laying his head back down, Kajsa put the cup back under the drip and put some more wood on the fire. I will go in the morning; now I will boil my berries! She said to herself.

A crash of thunder made her get up and walk to the cave's opening. Dark clouds had formed and were quickly moving her way. She could see lightning flashes and, a little while later, the crash of more thunder.

"Going to be a bad one," she said quietly, glad that she had stockpiled plenty of firewood. Finished with that task, Kajsa sat down and looked out the cave at the lightning. "I am here, Pappa. Come and get me," she whispered.

Chapter 17
Lübeck

The voyage was as expected, Pehr hanging over the rail during the day and lying with a wooden bucket beside him at night. He would heave until his stomach was empty, breathe deeply and begin to feel better. Then, he would have some soup and be okay for as long as the sea was calm. The first sign of weather and Pehr would run for the rail. Weak as a kitten, he gingerly made his way down the gangplank at the Lübeck docks. It took all his restraint not to fall to his hands and knees and kiss the ground.

Due to his last-minute departure, he had no chance to send word to Otto's shop or Horst's stable of his impending visit. He had been worried about how Otto would receive him as Pehr had promised Otto he would return after three fortnights to continue working for him when he left Lübeck so many years ago.

His first task was to find a restaurant. After that, he would need to purchase some clothes and find a room with a bath. Pehr still could not get used to the idea that he was a wealthy businessman. His shoemaking shop was a huge success with orders that would take months, if not years, to fill. He was advised by Axel to charge a premium for his shoes 'because they are premium shoes!' Raising his prices had not dampened sales and, after a year, he raised the prices again hoping to reduce the backlog in orders. It did not work, but it did accomplish one thing — his clientele was now mainly among Norway's elite.

So, with an obscene amount in gold and silver coins in his pocket, Pehr took a room at an impressive stone building that housed one of the finest hotels in all of Lübeck, according to a well-dressed man who looked dubiously at Pehr. "It is very expensive," he made sure to add. The man behind the desk sniffed pompously when Pehr walked up to the counter.

"Deliveries are in the back of the hotel!"

"I want a room," Pehr said, feeling insulted by the man's assumption.

"I am sorry, sir. We have no rooms available. Perhaps you would be more comfortable at one of the boarding houses down by the docks?"

"Nein!" Pehr said, taking a sack of gold ducats out of his trouser pocket and making a show of counting them.

"Perhaps I spoke too soon, sir!" the man stammered. "I remember our best suite became available just this morning!"

It took great self-control not to blanch when the man told him what the price was per night.

"I will also need a tailor and a hot bath," Pehr said.

"Of course, sir!" the man gushed, snapping his fingers for the bellhop.

"I have no luggage with me; my journey has been an ordeal."

"Of course, sir, quite understandable!" The man was practically falling over himself, trying to ingratiate himself to Pehr.

After being measured for two suits by a man the hotel concierge said was the best tailor in Lübeck, Pehr soaked in a hot bath, feeling the stress of the grueling voyage seep out of his pores. There was no privacy, however. Hotel staff was coming and going, fussing over the rich foreigner. After his bath, Pehr ordered sausages and sauerkraut with a liter of beer. The concierge paled at the request, but did not question him. Pehr had craved the traditional meal since setting foot back on Prussian soil again. Just to add to the concierge's discomfort, Pehr said, "The last time I entered Lübeck, I was destitute, hungry and wiping my arse with my fingers behind a horse stable!" The concierge paled, sniffed and left the room in the wake of Pehr's laughter.

After his meal, which took a while as his stomach kept clenching, Pehr lay down on the most comfortable bed he had ever lain on and fell into a deep sleep. He woke fourteen hours later, to bright sunlight coming through the floor to ceiling windows. He lay there thinking about the day in front of him.

"I should order some breakfast," he said aloud to himself.

"What would you like, sir?" The man appeared from nowhere, causing Pehr to jump.

"Skit! How long have you been standing in my room?"

"It is my duty to serve your every wish, sir. Now, may I suggest the eggs and bacon breakfast?"

"Bacon?" Pehr asked.

"Ja, it is smoked pork, very tasty, and, of course, some coffee?"

"Ja, coffee I know!"

The man disappeared while Pehr searched for the chamber pot. "It must be here somewhere!"

"What must be, sir?"

"Skit!" Pehr gasped, "Who are you?"

"I am here to serve, sir."

"Ach! Okay, I need to skit. Where do I do that?"

"Right in here, sir." The man showed Pehr a small room with

what looked like a dresser until he lifted the top. Set inside was a three-gallon crock under a carved wooden seat with a hole in it. To one side was a small washstand with a pitcher of water and a bowl. A small towel that looked softer than moss hung on a hook on the side of the stand.

"Tack" was all he could say. "You can leave now."

"I am here to serve, sir."

"I can wipe my own arse!" Pehr said, "and you will not want to be in this room in a few minutes, by gum!"

"Very good, sir!"

"Ah, what do I use to wipe my arse?" Pehr asked before the man left.

"Right here, sir." The man showed him a pile of cloth strips beside the washstand, hidden from view unless you were sitting on the toilet.

Afterward, Pehr came back into his room to see his bed made up and two new suits laid out. Someone had also polished his fine leather shoes. Getting dressed, he was impressed by the fit of the suit and the quality of the material. I wonder how much this will cost me, he thought and then braced himself for someone to jump out of nowhere and tell him. But he was quite alone. For some reason, Pehr felt a little disappointed.

After a delicious breakfast of eggs and bacon, washed down with fine coffee, Pehr decided the smoked meat was the tastiest thing he had ever eaten. No slight intended, Mamma! he thought.

He decided his first stop should be Horst's stables. Walking through the streets, he was amazed at the change in the city. There was an air of prosperity among the citizens, opposite of the post-war struggles the city went through when Pehr was last here. Men nodded to him and women smiled shyly at him. Pehr was always a good-looking man and age had further chiseled his features. The fine suit helped some too.

Some of the street names had changed, but from what he remembered, the stables should be where he now stood.

"Excuse me, sir," Pehr asked a passerby. "Could you tell me how to get to Horst's Stables?"

"Sorry, never heard of it."

"I remember a stable that used to stand where that house is now," another passerby offered. "Been gone five years at least."

"Do you know where the stable owner went?"

"Nein. Haven't seen him since."

Pehr stared at the house and yard, remembering all the visits he had with his old friend. With a sigh, he made his way to Otto's shoe store. The building was the same as it always was, the 'Shoes Repaired Here' sign and the dirty window being the only differences. A bell above the door clicked but did not ring as he entered. The smell of sweet pipe tobacco and leather he remembered had been replaced by a musty odor. A young man looked up from behind the counter. "Can I help you, sir?"

"Ja, is Otto here?"

"Otto?"

"Ja, Otto, the owner."

"Oh, him, nein. He sold the place to my uncle twelve or so years ago."

"Ja? What about Karl, the shoemaker?"

"Karl, was he the one who dropped dead one day walking back from the biergarten? Heart gave out, I heard. I think Otto sold the shop right after that."

"Is your uncle here?"

"Nein, he does not come here much anymore."

Pehr thanked the man and went in search of Sophia. Of course, the lady who answered the door at the house where Sophia had served as a maid did not know of anyone by that name. If only he could recall the fishmonger's name! He wandered down to the fish market, decidedly overdressed for the task. He got strange looks when he asked people if they knew of a fishmonger whose wife was named Sophia. After a fruitless hour, he wandered back to his hotel. So far, the journey was both disappointing and depressing. He felt sad for the death of his old friend Karl, remembering the banter he would have with him as he learned his craft, running to the biergarten for his pail of beer and sharing sausage and sauerkraut almost daily. He wondered if Karl's diet and beer consumption had anything to do with his demise. 'Nej, probably just old age. I should go to the biergarten this evening and have some more sausage and drink some beer in Karl's honor!'

After a short nap, Pehr walked to the biergarten, being led by the familiar aroma. He took a seat on one of the long benches, nodding at the couple sitting across from him.

"What will it be?" the server asked.

"Ein paar würstel und sauerkraut, bitte (a pair of sausage and sauerkraut, please)."

"Bier?"

"Ja."

Watching the solid-looking woman with the ample behind walk away, he sensed something familiar about her.

"Are you new to Lübeck, sir?" the man across the table asked.

"Nej, nein, I was here many years ago."

"Swedish?"

Here Pehr hesitated. The man looked as though he had been

a soldier sometime in his past and he was always careful, not knowing if there was any lingering animosity from the war.

"Norsk."

"Ahh, well, welcome, my friend!" The man and his wife lifted their steins and all Pehr could do was smile and nod back. He watched as the server brought two handfuls of steins filled to the rim and set them down in front of a large group of patrons without spilling a drop. He was admiring her ability when he felt the shock of recognition. Sophia? The years had not been kind to her, beefier and haggard-looking with a weary look etched in her face. She worked her way over to his spot and set the stein down.

"Sophia?"

"Ja?" She looked at him, waiting for him to continue. Then her eyes widened in recognition. "Pehr?"

"Ja!" Pehr cried, beginning to rise when she put a beefy hand on his shoulder, easing him back down.

"Your sausages will be here soon," she said brusquely and walked away.

Stunned, Pehr watched her take another patron's order and disappear through the kitchen door. Another server brought him his sausages and he asked her where Sophia was. She replied that she became ill and had to leave, eying him suspiciously.

Did Sophia harbor bitter feelings because Pehr never returned from his trip to Sweden so many years ago? But why would she be? She was to begin married life with the fishmonger after he left. Did she see him as a father figure, one who left, never to be seen again until now? He had to talk with her if he was ever to be at peace with himself, explain to her what had happened and why he put off returning until now.

Why had he put off returning for so long? Sure, he was

building his business and his seasickness was a reason, however sorry an excuse that was. He realized that he had no excuse, other than he had put this part of his life behind him. His appetite gone, Pehr left the biergarten, intending to go back to the hotel. As he was walking along the side of the biergarten, he glanced down the alley and spotted Sophia rounding the corner at the far end. Jogging to catch up, he turned the corner just as Sophia turned down the next street. For reasons he did not know, Pehr did not call after her. He kept his distance without losing sight of her, ready to hide if she glanced back.

He was in a rough part of the city now and stood out like a sore thumb. He was aware of the looks he was getting from some of the young men sitting on stairs in front of run-down shacks. Finally, Sophia turned into a decrepit shack — a hovel more accurately. He eased up near the shack and could hear loud voices and children screaming and crying through an open window. From what he could gather, the man was berating her for losing wages by leaving work early, followed by Sophia complaining about his drinking and neglecting the care of their children. This was followed by a loud slap and then the man storming out the front door, slamming it with great force for effect.

"Are you lost?"

Turning, Pehr saw that three tough-looking men had come up behind him without a sound.

"Nej, I am not lost."

"Then what are you doing here, with all these fine clothes and fancy shoes?"

"They look about my size," another added.

"Rolf!" Sophia yelled out the window. "I have enough trouble without you bothering der polizist [the policeman]." She looked at Pehr and said, "I suppose you're here looking for Ernst. Well, he's not here, but come on in and say your peace and begone with you!"

The three men reluctantly walked away, disappointed at losing an easy mark yet wary of provoking the police.

Pehr walked into the shack, appalled by the smell and condition of the place. Filth was everywhere, the smell of human feces overpowering. Four children ranging in age from five to eleven stared at him with hostile eyes.

"Say your peace and begone with you!"

"What happened, Sophia? Why are you angry at me?"

"Look around at what you left me to!" she screamed at him, spittle hitting his face.

"This is not my doing, Sophia!" Pehr cried.

"You left me!"

"I'm sorry, Sophia. I was robbed and left for dead in Norway," Pehr said softly. "It was many months before I recovered and I was left with nothing."

"Well, you don't look poor now!" She spat.

Pehr sighed and took a sack of silver coins out of his vest pocket and set it on the table with a clink. He did not look back when he left. He spent the next few days in his hotel room waiting for the return voyage to Trondheim. The concierge was all too happy to have a bellhop run to the apothecary for some ether and to the market for some ginger root and sugar lumps. Perhaps his voyage home would be a little more pleasant.

Chapter 18
September 15, 1777

The search for Kajsa was delayed by a severe thunderstorm. Hail the size of eggs fell from the skies and littered the farmyard. High winds followed, whipping trees back and forth and with rain coming sideways, hitting the cabin with such force, they worried about the windows. Katarina, Lovisa and the girls placed pots and pans wherever rain leaked through the sod-covered roof, but it was not enough. Water dripped in several places unprotected by containers. The pots and pans required constant emptying, tossing their contents through an open window on the leeward side of the cabin.

Olof slept through the wind and the noise. He lay on the bed, in his 10th hour of deep sleep, snoring with an open mouth, oblivious to all that was happening around him. That was until a drip formed directly above him, landing in his open mouth. Turning on his side didn't help, the drip landing in his ear canal. Opening his eyes, he could see his wife and daughters running back and forth with containers. He lay there puzzling the situation out when it all came back to him. His little Kajsa was missing!

Olof bolted up out of bed and was immediately hit with a dizzy spell. Sitting on the edge of the bed with his head bowed, he heard Stina yell, "Pappa's awake!"

Poking her head into the bedroom, Katarina asked, "How are you feeling, husband?"

"Better. Any sign of Kajsa yet?"

"Nothing. Toby and the Sámi are holed up in the barn and Lovisa is helping with the roof leaks."

"I will help," Olof said, rising from the bed and swaying a little.

"You sit at the table; there is lots of porridge left since the storm started before the men could come to eat," Katarina commanded.

Olof returned the smile Lovisa gave him as she hurried by with an overflowing pan. She was happy to see he had recovered from his fall into the water the day before. She had feared his shivering and loss of consciousness was something far more serious than just exhaustion.

Olof's stomach grumbled at the thought of hot porridge; it had been a while since his last meal.

"Pappa!" his girls all cried, running to him, hugging him and then leading him to the table by his hands, all chattering at once about the storm. Olof sat as they fussed over him, placing a bowl of porridge, a cup of water and a plate of knäckebröd before him.

"Girls, come help!" Katarina called as she walked swiftly past with an overflowing pot. It was chilly in the cabin and Olof glanced over at the hearth. Smoke from the log embers rose straight up the chimney. Olof suspected that the high winds caused an overdraft on the fire, gutting the flames and drawing all the heat up the chimney. Candles were burning throughout the cabin, but they provided little heat. Olof heard a shuffling noise and looked down. Jager was slowly dragging himself by his front paws toward Olof. When he got to him, Olof reached down and petted the dog's head. He realized the dog had been injured while trying to find his daughter and he felt a surge of compassion for him. So much so that he started to sob quietly. This caused Jager to whine, which caused Brita to glance over at them.

"Pappa's crying," she whispered to her mother.

Altogether, Katarina and her daughters went to Olof and knelt beside him or stood and hugged him, all soon reduced to tears. Lovisa stood and watched this all unfold, noting Jager's whining and nudging of Olof's leg. They seemed to be drawn together, the casualties of the last search. Jager had not regained the use of his hind legs yet although his tail twitched now and then.

Clearing her throat and wiping her eyes, Lovisa returned to the task of emptying the pots and pans. The rain and wind seemed to be letting up some; she hoped it would end soon so they could get back to the search. But she knew any tracks would be obliterated with this hail and rain and they would not have the dogs to assist them. It has now been seven days since Kajsa disappeared and Lovisa had to admit to herself that the chances of finding her alive were unlikely. Tears filled her eyes as she thought of Kajsa, delivering her on a sparkling spring day in April ten years past. She didn't have as many visits with Olof's children as she had with Emanuel's, but she loved Kajsa as much as any of her other nieces and nephews.

The rain and wind let up late afternoon, forcing them to postpone the search until the next morning. Tobias, Nikko and Jan braved the wind and rain, running from the barn to the cabin. Stina was standing by a window watching them as they ran, all tilting to one side as the wind whipped their coats and then, the wind suddenly stopped and all three went down in a heap in the muddy yard. The wind only stopped for a second though. The men got back to their feet, helping each other back up, soaked through and mud streaked. Stina laughed so hard the others ran to see what she was laughing at and they all began laughing as the men staggered and jogged sideways with each gust of wind. They all fell a few more times before grabbing a porch column and pulling themselves onto the porch. Lovisa opened the door when they were close and pulled them in one by one before shutting and barring the door behind them.

"Katarina, could you grab some blankets?" Lovisa called as she helped Tobias out of his coat. "We have to get that fire going!"

"I will fix that," Olof said, rising from his chair after one last scratch behind Jager's ear. Olof soon had the fire roaring, heat radiating throughout the room.

"Come over here and strip off those wet clothes!" Lovisa commanded. Giggles from the three girls as they stood transfixed, waiting for the show to begin.

"You girls get in the bedroom until they are finished. Go now!" Olof said with raised voice. The girls walked quickly out of the room, Anna and Brita peeking at the men one last time before entering the bedroom. The men sat in front of the fire after they had stripped down and wrapped a blanket around themselves. They still had mud-caked hair and streaked faces as they sat shivering. Katarina handed each of them a bowl of porridge. "It's cold. Sorry," she said.

"Tack!" they all said before shoveling the porridge into their famished bodies.

"I'll wash these clothes; we do have plenty of water in the house," Katarina said.

"Ja, they will dry fast enough with that fire blazing away," Lovisa added. It had gotten uncomfortably warm, but she was grateful for it as Tobias finally stopped shivering. She looked around for Olof and saw him sitting on the floor with Jager's head in his lap.

"You have made a friend, Olof," she said.

"Ja, will you be taking him when you go back home?"

"I don't know. He may be a burden on the camp when we travel between pastures," Lovisa said. "What do you think, Nikko, Jan?"

"If Olof wants him, he may be better off here," Jan said. Nikko nodded in agreement. Both knew Jager's purpose was to protect the herd by chasing down predators. Something he could no longer do.

"Ja, I will keep him, by gum!" Olof said.

There was a chorus of muffled 'yays' from behind the bedroom door.

"You can come out here, girls," Olof called. The bedroom door flew open and the girls ran over to Jager, showering him with hugs and kisses. Jager basked in the attention, panting in the heat with what looked like a grin on his face.

*****

The next morning, an hour before sunup, Olof, Lovisa, Tobias, Nikko and Jan were on the trail heading for the site of the dog's attack. The rain had stopped around midnight and the trail was muddy with large pools of water in low areas and depressions in the trail. Some places, they had to lead the horses over the slippery ground. Other areas, they had to skirt large ponds by walking on the grass bordering the trail, but the wet grass quickly soaked the bottoms of their pants. The hope was that the sun would come out and dry the ground, but it looked like it was going to be an overcast and dreary day ahead of them. There was a light wind though that would help the drying process.

Once again, Nikko and Jan were tasked with holding the horses when they arrived at the slope where they would leave the trail. They tied the horses to saplings and then went in search of dry wood for a fire. Olof, Lovisa and Tobias stood contemplating the hill before them.

"Is it possible?" Tobias asked. "It looks slipperier than snot on a doorknob."

"Toby!" Lovisa cried as Olof grinned.

"Sorry, Mamma."

"Only one way to find out," Olof said. "Toby, take this rope and see if you can make it to the tree right there." He was pointing at a poplar tree about 15 feet up the slope.

Tobias nodded and tied one end of the rope around his waist, leaving the rest to trail behind him. Olof went to the horses and brought back more coils of the hemp rope and handed them to Tobias. "For the next trees."

Tobias nodded, put his arms through the coils of rope and hitched them up onto his shoulders. He then took a deep breath and ran up the slope, slipping in spots but grabbing saplings or any plants available to keep from sliding back down. Once he made it to the poplar tree, he removed the rope from his waist and tied it securely to the tree. He then looked up the slope for his next tree, planning his ascent by the saplings between him and his target. Pushing off the tree, he crab-crawled up to the next tree. He repeated the process until he came to a flat shelf and called down to his mother and uncle to come on up. Their ascent was easier than Tobias's with the rope to pull themselves up. After they all were standing on the shelf, Tobias said, "I found

Raul over this way." He pointed to the east.

They found what was left of Raul. Scavengers and carrion eaters had picked away at him. Fur and bone remained, his skull devoid of eyes or tongue. The sight broke Lovisa's heart, dear Raul, her devoted friend.

Lovisa and Tobias took the time to bury Raul as best they could as Olof waited impatiently.

"Rest well, Raul," Lovisa said quietly. "You did your best."

After a few seconds, Lovisa stood and walked over to Olof.

"The dogs were heading in a north-easterly heading so we should keep climbing in that direction," Olof said.

"It may be quicker to follow this shelf around this hill than trying to go over it," Lovisa countered.

"What if she is up there?" Olof said, pointing up the incline. There were another hundred yards of slope to go before they would crest the hill.

"I can continue climbing and you two can go around, so we don't miss anything," Tobias suggested.

"Ja, that is good," Olof replied, looking at Lovisa for agreement.

"Okay, but be careful, Toby."

"Ja, I will," he said and then loped up the hill, grabbing the sapling he was aiming for. Olof grinned at Lovisa, proud of his nephew. It had been eight days since Kajsa had been missing and, even though Olof didn't realize it, he was well into the grieving stage, being able to grin and to find some happiness for the gift of Jager.

"Let's go, brother," Lovisa said and started walking along the shelf. Olof watched her walk away, nodded and said quietly, "Ja, it is good." He didn't think Lovisa heard him, but she smiled as she continued walking. The rock shelf they were walking on came to an abrupt end after a hundred yards. "What should we do, Olof?"

"I guess we go up."

"Ja, that is what I was thinking. It is not as steep here and we should be able to go at it on an angle instead of straight up," Lovisa said. The sun was still hidden behind the low bank of gray clouds, clouds that threatened more rain.

They came around a bend near the top of the hill and were met by Tobias.

"I could hear you two grunting from a half-mile away, so I thought I better come check on you!" Tobias said when they approached him.

"That was Olof," Lovisa said, trying not to pant. "He is not as young as your mother!"

"Hah!" Olof countered, "It was not I who shrieked every time I slipped!"

"There is a trail down there, between this hill and the base of that mountain," Tobias said, pointing down the slope.

"Where? I don't see anything," Olof said, squinting in the direction Tobias was pointing.

"I see it," Lovisa said. "Looks like an animal trail."

"Where?" Olof asked.

"Come on. Let's go have a look," Tobias said, not bothering to respond to Olof. He dropped onto his rear and slid down the slope, grabbing saplings now and then to slow his descent.

"Skit!" Olof cried, "Doesn't he know we are no longer young?"

"Speak for yourself, old man!" Lovisa cried as she dropped on her rear, a little harder than she meant to, and followed

Tobias's slide down.

"Skit!" Olof muttered as he gently eased to a sitting position and pushed off with a little too much force. He rocketed down the hill, missing the saplings he reached for, and careening into Lovisa halfway down the hill. They both continued the slide in a free fall, hanging onto each other, Lovisa hoping she would not be on the bottom when they came to a stop. They hit a sapling, Olof taking the full brunt of it square in the back, causing him to grunt, "Oof." It did slow their descent down enough for Lovisa to extricate herself from Olof, pushing away with her feet. Olof hit the bottom first and started to say, "That was …." when the breath was knocked out of him by Lovisa plowing into his midsection.

"Are you okay, Olof?" Lovisa asked.

"Uh, huh, huh!" Olof gasped, trying to fill his lungs with air. In the background, Lovisa could hear Tobias as he tried to suppress his laughter.

"That's not funny, Toby!" she said.

"Ja? It may just be about the funniest thing I have ever seen!"

Chapter 19
Kajsa

Kajsa built up the fire and laid some logs close to hand for Jäkel. She also placed a full cup of water beside him. She gagged when she bent down to place the cup, smelling the open wound on his leg. Covering her nose, she bent down behind him to examine the wound. The sight of it was too much for her and she vomited what little she had in her stomach. The wound had turned black and wet with tiny bubbles and smelled like rotting meat.

After vomiting, Kajsa fell back on her rear and scrabbled a few feet back. This is bad! she thought. I better go get help right now! Standing, she said, "I have to leave now, Jäkel." He raised one hand in a feeble, beckoning motion. He appeared feverish. Kajsa inched closer but maintained a safe distance from the smell. He slurred something she couldn't hear.

"What was that, Jäkel?"

"My name is Dánel," he whispered. The stench of his breath was no match for the stench of his wound, but it was close.

"Okay, Dánel, I will go get help."

"Nej, little one. Let me die here."

"I can't do that, Jäkel, er, Dánel."

"You have to; they will cut off my leg and after that, they will shoot me." He gasped and then fell back and closed his eyes. His breathing was shallow and labored and his face was flushed and sweaty. Kajsa studied him for a while and then stood and walked out of the cave. She made her way down to the trail, turned right and began walking. After several hundred yards, she came to a sudden stop. Was that voices she heard, listening intently? Then she heard movement off to her left. Someone or something was crashing through the brush. Then she could hear people arguing.

"Watch out, Toby. That willow almost took my eye out!"

"Sorry, Olof, but you shouldn't walk so close behind me."

"Ach, then get a move on!"

"I have to pick my way through here; all you have to do is follow my trail!"

"Boys!" Lovisa cried. "Stop acting like children! Toby, trade places with Olof for a while!"

"Ja, Mamma."

"Pappa?"

They all froze when they heard the voice coming from somewhere in front of them. The willows were thick and most stood 12 feet or higher.

"Kajsa?" Olof yelled, daring to believe it was her that called.

"Ja, Pappa, you came!"

Olof pushed past Tobias and crashed headlong through the willows, branches scratching his face that he didn't feel. He emerged on the trail and Kajsa ran into his arms, Olof lifting her in a bear hug. "I knew you would come for me, Pappa; I called for you every night," she whispered in his ear.

"Are you okay, Kajsa?" Olof asked hoarsely.

"Ja, I am okay," she said.

Lovisa and Tobias came out of the willows and onto the trail.

"Kajsa, is it really you?" Lovisa said.

"Auntie, Toby!" Kajsa cried over Olof's shoulder. Neither one of them was ready to let go of each other yet, so Lovisa and Tobias stood smiling at them with tears in their eyes. Lovisa put her arm around Tobias and squeezed.

"What happened, Kajsa?" Lovisa asked.

"Jäkel, I mean Dánel, took me and locked me in a cave, but I climbed out through the top of the cave and jumped on to a tree and climbed down. Then Jäkel was lying there with his leg torn open and then I took care of him and then I left!" She stopped to catch her breath as they looked at her with stunned expressions.

"Dánel?" Lovisa stammered, "Did you say Dánel?"

"Ja, I called him Jäkel, but he is not a Jäkel."

"Where is he?" Lovisa asked, "Is he still alive?"

"Ja, not too far. Back this way." Kajsa nodded her head back over her shoulder.

"Can you take us there, Kajsa?" Lovisa asked, looking at Olof for permission.

"Ja, he needs help. I will take you to him," Kajsa said. Olof nodded and started walking, holding Kajsa's hand as they walked.

"Pappa?"

"Ja?"

"He didn't touch me." Olof began sobbing then, stopping and kneeling on the ground.

"It's okay, Pappa."

All he could do was nod his head until he composed himself. Lovisa and Tobias kept a respectful distance from them.

"Okay, let's go see this Jäkel," he said as he stood and started walking again.

When they came to the mouth of the cave, Lovisa looked at Olof and said, "Toby and I will go inside."

"Nej, I have business with this monster!" Olof growled,

clearly furious at this man for taking his daughter.

"He is my man and Toby's father, stepfather," Lovisa said, her hand on his chest to stop him from advancing into the cave. "Let us go first and then you can go after."

Olof looked at Lovisa, saw the pleading in her eyes and nodded. He was clearly furious, his body visibly shaking with rage as he walked to the edge of the shelf and stared out at the vista before him. Kajsa walked up beside him and took his hand. They stood like that without talking.

Lovisa and Tobias walked carefully into the cave both alert to any hidden danger in this unfamiliar and enclosed place. Seeing the form lying beside a small fire near the back of the cave, they walked slowly up to it with knife and hatchet drawn. Tobias signaled Lovisa to circle around behind the man while Tobias circled around the front.

"Is it him?"

"Ja, it's him," Tobias answered. He moved nearer and nudged Dánel's knee on his good leg. He did not stir. Kneeling in front of Dánel, Tobias kept his knife at the ready as he put the back of his hand in front of Dánel's nose and open mouth. After a few seconds, he stood and said, "He's dead." Lovisa nodded. She didn't feel any emotions as she had already grieved his death. She was looking at the torn, festering wound on Dánel's thigh, wondering if it was Jager or Raul that inflicted the bite.

When they walked out of the cave, Olof strode purposely toward the cave's mouth, where Lovisa stopped him. "He's dead." Olof stood, breathing heavily, trying to suppress his rage for his daughter's sake. "I need to see it," he said through clenched teeth. Lovisa stepped aside and said to Tobias, "Come, we must make a platform and gather some firewood."

"Why?" Kajsa asked. She had been standing and watching the interaction between her father and Lovisa, sobbing quietly.

"What's wrong, min älskling?" Lovisa said, going to her and enveloping her in a hug. "You are safe now; he won't bother you anymore."

"I didn't want him to die!" Kajsa sobbed.

Olof came out of the cave and walked up to them. "Let's go home," he said quietly.

"You two go ahead, Olof," Lovisa said. "Toby and I have to prepare his body." She didn't mention that they were going to burn his body, for Kajsa's sake. Olof looked at her and Tobias and nodded. "Tack for your help in finding Kajsa," he said as he shook Tobias's hand. When he tried to shake Lovisa's hand, she pulled him in and hugged him. Turning to Kajsa, she knelt and hugged her too. "Tack, Auntie," Kajsa whispered. She went to Tobias and hugged him also.

"Let's go, Pappa!" she said. "I'm so hungry, I could eat a whole cow!"

"A whole cow, you say?" Olof said as they walked away.

"Ja, and the hooves too!"

"The hooves too. You really are hungry."

"And I need a bath too."

"Do you now?" Olof said, "I just thought you wrestled with a skunk!"

"Pappa!"

"Maybe you can bath with Jager. I think he needs a bath too."

"Ugh, I'm not bathing with a boy!"

"Jager is a dog. Lovisa gave him to us."

"We have a dog?" Kajsa shrieked.

"Ja, he is hurt though. His back legs won't move."

"Really, what happened to him?"

"An accident. He was helping the search for you when he got hurt."

"I'm sorry; I will look after him!"

Lovisa stood watching them walk away and listening to their conversation with a smile on her face. When they got out of hearing range, Lovisa said, "Okay, Toby, let's get this done."

* * * *

Jager did not regain full use of his hind legs. Olof built a little chair with wheels on the back for him. He would set Jager's back end on the chair and then Jager could walk around the farm with his front legs while the wheels carrying his back end would roll along behind him. He got around as easily as he could when he had four working legs. Olof had cut an opening in the bottom of the chair where Jager could relieve himself whenever necessary. Although the Raderman girls fussed over Jager, he was devoted to Olof and the two of them could be seen walking around the farmyard together as Olof went about his daily chores. Katarina would often think of her father-in-law, Olaus and his pig, Annika. Those two were always together, walking around the farm together much the same way as Olof and Jager did now.

Kajsa didn't have any lasting effects from her capture and escape other than having to relate the story numerous times to everyone from the Pastor to her friends and cousins. Her celebrity was short-lived though as everyone soon got back to their everyday routines. She did develop a close attachment to her father, always wanting to go with him whenever he left the farm. Her mother attributed that to her fear of being kidnapped again.

Chapter 20
Summer 1778

Maria Emanuelsdotter was once again visiting her cousins, Kajsa and Stina. The girls had discovered a swimming hole not far from the Raderman home where the boys from neighboring farms went to swim on hot days. The girls had crept up to a clearing, where the boys had undressed, and hid among a cluster of willows. It had come as a shock when they noticed that the boys had stripped down to nothing before jumping into the water.

Their reactions began with revulsion, changed to giggling, then fascination.

"They stick that floppy thing in your peepee when you get married, Maria," Stina whispered.

"Nej!" Maria breathed. "I am never getting married! What are those other things?"

"I don't know."

They were quiet for a while, each deep in their own thoughts.

"They look like little sacks; maybe they keep stuff in them?" Stina asked.

"Ugh, what would they keep in there?" Kajsa said.

"I don't know," Maria said. "Come on, let's take their clothes and leave them at the other end of the road!"

"Ja!"

They crept forward, suppressing their giggles, gathered all the boy's clothes and crept back, undetected. They then ran to the road, walked past a few farmhouses, deposited them at the edge of the road and then walked arm in arm, laughing all the way back to Kajsa and Stina's home.

An hour later, Lars Larsson, Israel Håkansson, Gunnar Johansson and Gösta Mårtensson emerged from the pond and lay on the clearing's grass to dry themselves in the sun.

"Who are you thinking about, Gösta?" Gunnar asked with a grin.

"Eh? Oh, skit!" Gösta said, covering his arousal with his hands. "Damn thing has a mind of its own!"

The boys, aged twelve to thirteen, burst out laughing at Gösta's predicament.

"Hey, where are my clothes?" Israel demanded.

"Ja, mine too!" Lars added.

"Someone took our clothes!" Gunnar cried. The boys all covered themselves with their hands and looked around them for any sign of the perpetrator, or perpetrators. The situation did have a positive effect on Gösta, who still hid himself, but the hiding was not as hard as it was a few seconds earlier. The boys searched the bushes around the clearing in a growing panic. The gravity of their situation dawned on them as they found no trace of their clothes.

"What do we do, Lars?" asked Gunnar. Lars was the unofficial leader of the group; they all looked to him for direction when faced with situations.

"I don't know, Gunnar," he replied. "We may have to wait for it to get dark."

"It only gets dark for a few hours, in the middle of the night!" Israel said. "And I have to help my father after dinner!"

"Okay." Lars thought for a minute, then said, "We will break off spruce branches to cover ourselves and then make a run for it."

"That is good thinking, Lars!" Gösta said.

They set about breaking off branches, one for the front and one for the rear. They walked gingerly on bare feet through the trail toward the road and stopped to look both ways.

"Nothing. Should we make a run for it?" Gunnar asked.

"Let's make sure there is no one coming," Lars said. "There's nowhere to hide once we get on the road."

"Gösta!" Israel asked, "Are you thinking about my grandmother again?"

"Huh," Gösta asked, not comprehending, then looking down. "Skit!"

He was, once again, fully aroused. The others laughed again; Gösta was always thinking and talking about girls.

"Okay," Lars ordered, "let's go!"

They ran out into the road, trying to keep the spruce boughs in place. The road, more sand than dirt, was two worn tracks where wagon wheels rolled and a strip of grass down the middle.

"These hurt like hell whenever they touch me!" Gunnar whined, and then flung his spruce boughs aside. Walking down the road, the others soon followed suit, which came as a shock to the parish Pastor and his wife, whose horse and buggy crested a hill in the road. The boys, not knowing what to do as they approached the buggy, slowed to a walk and put their heads down and covered their privates as best they could, mumbling, "God eftermiddag [good afternoon] Pastor, Ma'am." Gösta didn't try very hard to hide himself and grinned at the preacher's wife as they passed. The Pastor was too flabbergasted to reply. His wife feigned shock, but she did not look away, and even, much to her husband's dismay, turned to look at their retreating backsides. Gösta turned around fully erect and winked at the parson's wife, causing her to smile. They could hear the parson admonishing his wife as they continued on their way.

"We will hear about this from our fars [fathers]!" Lars said.

"Our clothes!" Gunnar cried, spotting them strewn on the side of the road.

They all broke into a run but came up short when Lars yelled, "Stop!"

"Why?" Gunnar asked.

"Let's see if there are any footprints."

"Ja, good idea, Lars!" Israel said.

They walked slowly toward their clothes, all eyes scanning the ground.

"There, three sets of footprints, small, like children's, and barefoot," Lars observed.

"Let's follow them!" Gösta said, clearly excited.

"Ja, but first, let's get dressed!" Gunnar said. "I'm tired of seeing your cuk flopping around!"

After dressing, which Gösta seemed reluctant to do, they followed the footprints in the dirt road for a hundred yards before they veered off the road and onto a grassed trail.

"Where does that trail go?" Lars asked no one in particular.

"To the Emanuelsson farm," Israel said. "I know who did this."

"Stina and Kajsa?" Lars asked.

"Ja, and probably Maria too," Israel answered. "Those three are always together and getting into trouble."

"What are we going to do, Lars?" Gunnar asked.

"I don't know. Let me think on it," Lars said. "I've got to get home before the Pastor shows up, and pretend I was there all day."

"Ja, that is a good idea!"

They all bolted in different directions, eager to get home before the Pastor showed up. Lars and Gunnar had to go back the way they came while Gösta and Israel continued down the road toward their homes. Lars had no illusions that he could beat the pastor to his farm. His only hope was that the pastor stopped at Gunnar's farm first.

*＊＊＊

Lars crept behind the barn at his family's farm, climbing on top of the lean-to. There was a rectangular vent that was loose enough for him to pry off, something he and his friends discovered the year previous. Climbing through the opening, he stepped onto the barn's loft. Grasping the vent through its slats, Lars pulled the vent back onto its frame. Giving it a good tug, the remaining nails slid back into their old holes.

The loft floor was two-inch-thick rough sawn planks strewn with straw. Lars walked quietly to the ladder and lay down with his head over the opening. Peering down, he did not see any activity in the barn. As quietly as he could, he descended the ladder. He just set his foot on the barn's dirt floor when he felt a powerful hand grasp his shoulder in a painful grip. Turning his head, he looked directly into his father's angry face.

Laurits Pehrsson was a hard-working farmer, the son of a hard-working farmer, who was also a son of a hard-working farmer. He, his son and his father were all named Lars, so to avoid confusion, he was called Laurits, at least among family and friends. Laurits brokered no idleness; work was the only activity a man was supposed to do during his waking hours, other than taking meals, and, of course, his matrimonial duties.

"The pastor stopped by with a story of naked boys walking down the road!" he said, still keeping a painful hold on his son's shoulder, "and with his wife in the buggy! Would you know anything about that?"

Here was a test, Lars knew. Tell the truth and face the punishment or tell a lie and face punishment for lying and for the transgression. Lars decided to go with the truth.

"I went swimming with my friends and the Raderman girls stole our clothes!"

Laurits's lips twitched. "And?"

"And we didn't see the pastor's buggy until it came over the hill and then it was too late."

"And why were you sneaking down from the loft?"

Here was another test. Lars figured he ought to stick to the truth, emboldened by that twitch of his father's lips, hoping he was right in his assumption that it was suppressed humor.

"I was going to pretend I was here all afternoon," Lars said quietly, his head down, hoping he looked endearingly pathetic.

"Alright, you can go."

"Really!" Lars asked.

"Ja, you can go and cut a diamond willow for your whipping!"

"Ach!" Lars cried, then seeing his father's glare, "Ja, sir," he said, trudging out of the barn, rubbing his shoulder where his father had squeezed. He walked into the cottage, seeing his mother, Maria Svensdotter, at the stove. He said, "Hej, Mamma, I need a knife to cut a diamond willow."

Nodding, she said, "In the drawer. Bring it back before you go back to the barn."

"Ja, Mamma."

Walking out of the cabin, Lars's sister Märta asked, "Where is Lars going with that knife, Mamma?"

"To cut a willow."

"Why?"

"He did something bad and has to be punished."

"What did he do?"

"None of your concern, min älskling."

Märta, nine, scurried to the ledge below the front window, climbed up and looked out. She was soon joined by her sisters, Freda and Hannah, seven and five respectively. Three little faces pressed up against the glass looking at their big brother walking to a diamond willow bush. After Lars selected what he thought would be the least painful willow, he cut it and walked back to the cabin. He was going to put the knife back in the drawer when his mother stopped him. Lars had a brief flicker of hope when he thought his mother was going to intervene, but she said, "I need to wash that knife."

As Lars was walking out of the cabin with his willow, Märta cried, "Lars, don't go!"

He stopped at the door and said, "It's okay, Märta. I will be okay."

As he walked across the yard, three little girls were bawling at the window.

He was allowed to leave his pants on as he took his punishment. That cushioned much of the sting, but it still smarted with each strike. He was told the punishment was not for walking naked down the road, but for trying to hide his guilt. His father told him that he should always own up to his transgressions. He waddled back across the yard, seeing three tearstained faces watching him from the window. They crowded around him when he walked into the cottage, grabbing his hands and asking if he was okay. The three little girls fussed over their big brother throughout the evening meal, casting venomous glances at their father. Lars was quite enjoying the attention, being waited on, his cup refilled, food passed and dished up for him. He did set his limit when Hannah tried to spoon-feed him, much to his mother's amusement and to his father's annoyance.

"You can have my smulpaj [crumb pie], Lars," Freda said.

"You eat your own pie, Freda!" admonished her father.

"Ja, Pappa."

Chapter 21
Revenge

Lars, Israel, Gunnar and Gösta met the next day to compare punishments. Lars realized how easy he got off, compared to the punishment doled out to his friends. Gösta got the worst of it after the pastor told his father of Gösta's lewd look at his wife.

Gösta told his friends of his trip to the outhouse that morning. The blood from his whipping had dried overnight, cementing his underwear to the welts on his behind. Tearing the scabs when he peeled his underwear from his behind so he could empty his bowels was as painful as, if not more, than the original whipping.

"We need to get back at Pastor Silfversköld," Gunnar said. "He is responsible for our whippings!"

"Ja, but how?" Israel asked.

"I have an idea," Lars said, and then shared his plan with his friends. They listened, slowly nodding their heads and then grinning.

***

That night, after their families were asleep, the boys snuck out of their homes and met near Israel's farm, which was the last of their farms on the way to the parsonage. They came prepared, carrying two heavy boards, four lengths of hemp rope and several long willows. Nearing the parsonage, they circled around back of the property and came up behind the outhouse. Working as quietly as they could, and keeping an eye on the parsonage's windows, they tipped the front of the outhouse back until they could slide one of the boards underneath. Moving to the back, they tipped the outhouse forward and slid the other board underneath. This was harder than tilting the front as the structure was tilted back and gravity was working against them. Next, they looped a length of the rope around the ends of each board and slung the other over their shoulders. Lars and Israel were on one side and Gunnar and Gösta on the other. Lars counted down from three and each strained to lift the outhouse. Staggering under its weight, they stutter-stepped six feet before setting the small structure down.

Now the outhouse sat with its door at the edge of the sewage pit. After removing the boards, they laid willows over the open pit. Lars had to admonish them several times as they kept chuckling. They grabbed handfuls of long grass and spread them over the willows to conceal the pit underneath. Satisfied with their work, they crept back to the bush line to wait for the parson to make a trip to the outhouse.

After an hour or so, the boys were getting restless.

"Fek this!" Lars said, "I'm going home to sleep."

"Ja, me too," Gunnar agreed.

So it was that they left the parsonage at 4:00 a.m. It would be another hour before Pastor Silfversköld walked sleepily outside for his morning constitutional. He carried in one hand a lantern, and in the other, a full chamber pot. By the time he realized it was taking a few extra steps to reach the outhouse than usual, he was falling through the grass-covered willows into the sewage pit. The only saving grace was that it was a soft landing; the chamber pot's contents splashing him full in the face upon landing. The pastor's wife, preparing breakfast, was alarmed to hear her husband spouting some of the saltiest of profanities she had ever heard, and she who grew up near the docks of Umeå!

* * * *

All through the next day, Lars went about his chores with a feeling of anxiety, frequently looking down the lane leading into his farmyard whenever he walked through the courtyard. His anxiety spiked when he spotted the pastor's buggy coming down the lane. He made himself scarce, hiding in the barn, peeking through a knothole in one of the wallboards.

"Välkommen, Pastor!" Laurits called.

"Hej, Laurits," the pastor replied, his facial expression betraying his anger.

"What is it, Pastor?" Laurits asked. "You look upset."

"Your boy and his friends moved my outhouse back last night and I fell in the hole this morning!"

"Eh?" Laurits asked incredulously, "What is that you say?"

"Your boy and his friends," Pastor Silfversköld cried, "moved my outhouse back and I fell into skit!"

"Nej!" Laurits breathed, his mouth twitching as he pictured the pastor falling into his sewage pit.

"It is not a laughing matter, Laurits Pehrsson!" the parson said. "Bring him out so I can administer his punishment!" The pastor pulled his buggy whip out of the holder and started to climb down from his buggy. Laurits put his hand on the pastor's wrist, stopping him from climbing down.

"Nej, Pastor, you will not be administering any punishment to my son!" Laurits said quietly, "not here, nor in church." He squeezed the pastor's wrist while locking eyes with him until the parson winced. It also wasn't lost on the pastor when Laurits surreptitiously put his other hand under his nose. As hard as he had scrubbed in the bath his wife drew for him, the pastor could not entirely remove the lingering aroma of urine and feces from his body.

"Fine, but I will not be satisfied until you profess to me that sound punishment was delivered!" the parson said, trying his best to regain some semblance of authority. The pastor wheeled his buggy around and then whipped his horse into a gallop. Laurits stood in the dust, with his back to the barn. Lars watched him, not sure if his father was chuckling or coughing on the dust. Eventually, Laurits turned and stared directly at the knothole in the barn board, causing Lars to gasp and jump back.

Walking into the barn, his father said, "Lars, come here."

Lars walked slowly to his father and stopped several feet away.

"Ja, Pappa?"

"Did you and your friends move the pastor's outhouse off his sewage pit?"

Lars, remembering the whipping he got for trying to hide his guilt, said, "Ja, it was us."

Lars felt a surge of relief when he saw his father's lips twitch, but that was short-lived when his father said, "Okay, son, go cut me a diamond willow."

"Ja, Pappa." Lars said, "Pappa?"

"Ja?"

"The welts from the last whipping haven't healed yet."

"Ja?" Laurits said, "Okay, son, remind me next week to give you a whipping then."

"Ja!" Lars said enthusiastically, "I will!"

"Okay, get back to your chores now."

"Ja, Pappa!" Lars cried, running out of the barn, then slowing and feigning a limp.

He wasn't sure, but he thought he heard light chuckling from behind him. He wouldn't remind his father and his father seemed to have forgotten all about it when a week passed, even though the pastor mentioned the incident again the following Sunday.

The boys would meet up later that evening to compare notes. Lars was the only one to escape the willow. Gösta, once again, suffered the most, having his scabbed over welts torn open again with another whipping. He would have another painful removal of his underwear the next morning.

"Now, we need to come up with how we are going to get even with the Raderman girls for stealing our clothes!" Lars said.

"Can we wait until my bum heals before we do that?" Gösta groaned.

"Ach, I suppose!" Lars said.

*****

That Sunday's sermon did not begin well. The pastor started with:

"Let every person be subject to the governing authorities. For there is no authority except from God, and those that exist have been instituted by God. Therefore, whoever resists the authorities resists what God has appointed, and those who resist will incur judgment. For rulers are not a terror to good conduct, but to bad."

He then launched into:

"And have you forgotten the exhortation that addresses you as sons? 'My son, do not regard lightly the discipline of the Lord, nor be weary when reproved by Him. For the Lord disciplines the one He loves and chastises every son whom he receives."

And then:

"In the early morning hours of Thursday, June 11 in the year of our lord, 1778, four boys came to the parsonage and set a malicious trap for me." This caused some murmuring among the parishioners.

"I will now call up those four boys to receive God's punishment."

Laurits shot to his feet and hollered, "I have already administered punishment on my barn! There is no need for more!"

The fathers of Gunnar, Israel and Gösta also stood and all said, "As have I!"

"They have not been punished in the eyes of the Lord!" boomed the pastor.

"But as for me and my house, we will serve the Lord," Laurits responded.

"What trap did they set, father?" Gabriel Jonsson called from the back pews.

"The details of the trap are of no consequence!" Pastor Silfversköld yelled.

"Then how will we know if the punishment is just?" Gabriel replied.

Pastor Silfversköld was glaring at Gösta, who, above all other boys, he detested the most. The memory of him moving his hands away from his genitals and leering at his wife on the road that fateful day was burned into his memory.

"The boys moved my outhouse back, leaving the pit open for me to fall into!" he boomed.

"Did you?" Gabriel asked.

"Did I what?"

"Did you fall into the pit?"

The pastor muttered something under his breath and Gabriel called, "I did not hear you, Pastor!"

"Ja, I fell into the pit!" the pastor bellowed, his face flushing red.

Muffled chuckles ran through the assembled worshippers, the women included. The boys were grinning like heroes until Laurits cuffed his son across the back of his head. Laurits stood and said, "I would not object to my barn kneeling on the repentance board for the remainder of the sermon, Father." The other boy's fathers quickly voiced their agreement to the repentance board punishment.

Pastor Silfversköld was about to object, then realized Laurits was giving him an out. He did not want a confrontation with the four boy's fathers in front of his entire parish.

"I would agree; the punishment fits." The pastor announced, "Lars Larsson, Israel Håkansson, Gunnar Johansson and Gösta Mårtensson, step forward and remove your pants!"

Marie leaned into her husband and whispered into his ear. Laurits stood up and asked, "Why do they have to remove their pants, Pastor?"

"The repentance board is a punishment requiring bare knees," he replied. Laurits couldn't dispute that fact, so he pushed his son forward. All four boys made their way slowly to the front of the church and looked around behind them. They heard girls giggling and focused on Stina and Kajsa, with Maria right behind them, all covering their mouths, but that did not hide the fact that they were giggling. Scowling, Lars lowered his pants to his ankles and knelt on the hard, oaken plank. The other boys followed suit, all wearing cloth undergarments, except for Gösta, who wore nothing under his pants. Gasps, and giggles, came from the gathered females, and a scattering of chuckles from the men. The gasps were in response to seeing the angry welts on Gösta's backside.

The pastor harrumphed and proceeded to deliver what was the longest sermon in recent memory. It may not have lasted so long had the pastor looked to his left, where his wife was playing the piano during hymns. She was openly gaping at the front of Gösta's tunic. The material had lifted and stood out due to Gösta's rather large and obvious erection. The sight flustered the pastor, but he was determined to keep the boys on the repentance board as long as he could. More irritating to the pastor was the fact that he could not stop glancing at the bulge. At one point, Gösta noticed the pastor looking and then winked at him with a big grin when the pastor looked up at his face. The pastor flushed furiously but still could not help himself from glancing downward now and then, which only infuriated him more.

The snoring began in the second hour of the sermon. People were shifting, small children were fidgeting and several infants began to cry.

"Wrap it up, Pastor. My arse is getting sore!" Gabriel called. Laughter and a chorus of 'amens' convinced the pastor it was indeed time to end the sermon.

Chapter 22
The Courtship Begins

Part of the responsibilities of the rote farms was to provide the rote soldier with hay and seed. This year, that responsibility fell to Laurits Pehrsson. And so, it was that, after the harvest, Laurits and Lars traveled to the Raderman farm to supply Soldier Raderman with the year's allotment of hay and seed. Laurits did not mind this as it was a small price to pay for not having to serve in the army or to fight in lengthy wars. Laurits also brought with him Soldier Raderman's salary, collected from all the rote farmers.

"Välkommen, Laurits and Lars!" Olof greeted as they steered the wagon over to the barn.

"Hej, Olof!" Laurits responded, pulling the wagon brake back and winding the reins around the handle. They spent a few hours moving the hay from the wagon to the barn loft. It was a sufficient amount to feed Olof's cow and horse through the coming winter. The seed would be stored for the spring planting.

"You will stay for the evening meal," Olof said. It was more a statement than a request.

"Of course, Olof!" Laurits said. "I would not miss your wife's good cooking."

It was an annual exchange Olof had with the rote farmer whose turn it was to supply the hay, seed and delivery of salary that year. The outdoor dining table was laden with food for the men. Olof's wife, Katarina, and his daughters Brita, Kajsa and Stina, bustled in and out of the cabin carrying platters and pitchers. Lars sat across from Stina and Kajsa, who both whispered and giggled until their mother admonished them. Lars just scowled at them, then tried to ignore them. This became difficult when Kajsa stuck a carrot in each nostril and stared at him until he gave in and chuckled.

"Kajsa!" Olof said, "Stop that foolishness, and don't get up from the table until you eat those carrots!"

This brought a roar of laughter from Laurits, and soon everyone joined in. Kajsa kept trying to get Lars's attention and when she did, she would make funny faces, crossing her eyes or squishing her face. When all he would do was grin, she stepped it up a notch and put a finger under her eyelid on each side and a thumb at the corners of her mouth and squeezed together while crossing her eyes. The comical face was too much for Lars and he sprayed cider out his nose.

"That's it. If you kids can't be civilized, go play in the barn with the other animals!"

"Ja, Pappa!" the girls said and raced away from the table.

"You girls come back after playing and clean these dishes!" Katarina called.

The girls slowed and walked dejectedly to the barn.

"Well, go with them, boy!" Laurits said to his son.

Lars got up, turned to Katarina and said, "That was a delicious meal, Mrs. Raderman."

"Thank you, Lars."

He walked to the barn and peered inside. He didn't see anyone so he walked inside timidly. When he got to the center of the barn, the three girls rose up from behind straw bales and began firing cow chips at him. Lars covered his head and dove behind bales on the other side of the barn. He collected the chips thrown at him and began firing back at the girls. Squeals and laughter filled the air as the battle went on.

"Wait, Kajsa's got some in her eye!" Brita called.

Lars stopped throwing and walked over to them. "Are you okay, Kajsa?"

Kajsa had one hand over her eye and, when he got close, reared back and threw a moist cow chip right at him, followed by her sisters. Instead of retreating, Lar dove over the bales, setting the girls to shrieking. He caught Kajsa around her waist as Brita and Stina fled. They rolled until Lars found himself underneath her. Kajsa, flushed and holding his arms down, impulsively bent down and kissed him on his lips, then leaped up and ran out of the barn.

"You girls clean yourselves up and then get at those dishes!" Olof ordered. The adults were sitting on the porch, enjoying a cup of coffee. Lovisa had gifted a bag of coffee to them and they became addicted to the drink. Lars lay on the floor for a while, exhilarated by the kiss from Kajsa. He stumbled out of the barn in a daze. His father called, "Lars! Were you kicked by the cow?"

Lars walked over to them, a goofy look on his face, straw and cow dung in his hair. Kajsa was watching him with a smile on her face from the kitchen window.

"I don't want to know what those girls did to you, son, but it looks like you got the worst of it!" his father said. Olof and Katarina both grinned at this. "We should be going," Laurits said. "I thank you for the meal and the coffee."

"You are always welcome, Laurits," Katarina said. "Bring Maria next time."

"Ja, I will."

They rode out of the yard, Lars still with a goofy grin pasted on his face. He would later forbid his friends from exacting any revenge on the girls for the theft of their clothes.

Chapter 23
Summer 1782

The Great Coffee Venture

Olof and Emanuel Raderman, along with Erik Kiällberg, would meet every other Saturday at Olof's farm, behind the barn, to smoke their pipes, play checkers, recount battles won and lost and to drink coffee. That is until they ran out of coffee. Emanuel was the first to get hooked on the drink, courtesy of Lovisa. Since then, when he traded with the Sámi for meat, he would also trade for coffee beans. The Sámi traded with Norwegians near Trondheim for the beans, spices, salt and flour. In the past season, they were unable to trade for their usual amount, and therefore, Emanuel was only able to get half his usual amount.

"Have you tried Swedish coffee?" Erik asked.

"Ach," Olof spat, "that is pig swill!"

"What is that?" Emanuel asked.

"Gula mjölkhaltiga fröer [yellow milk vetch seeds]," Olof responded. "Fake coffee."

"And it tastes like coffee?"

"Nej, more like when you burp and some of your stomach juices come up."

"Ach, what are we going to do?" Erik asked.

"Do they sell it in Umeå?"

"Nej, you have to go to all the way to Stockholm to get coffee."

"Or Trondheim, in Norge," Emanuel said. "That is where the

Sámi trade for it."

"So, we could get coffee if we went to Trondheim, get all the coffee we want?" Olof asked.

"Ja, why?"

"If we went to Trondheim and traded for as much coffee as we could haul, we would have enough for us and we could sell the rest to shops in Umeå, at great profit!"

"Ja?"

"Ja!" Olof replied, chin out and nodding sagely. At fifty-two, he was the oldest of their little trio and, therefore, the wisest. At least to his way of thinking.

"What would we trade for the coffee?" Erik asked.

They all looked down at the checkerboard, puffing on their pipes, in deep thought for several minutes.

"The pigs!" Erik cried.

"Nej, not the pigs!" Olof said, appalled at the idea. The three of them had embarked on a joint venture: breeding and selling pork to the shops in Umeå and trading some to the Sámi. So far, it had proven modestly profitable for the three old soldiers. A few years earlier, Emanuel and Erik were forced to sell their sawmill after a larger sawmill set up operations near their territory. The interlopers were part of a lumber company with several sawmills throughout northern Sweden and they severely undercut Emanuel and Erik's lumber prices. In the end, Emanuel and Erik were forced to sell the sawmill to cover their mounting debt. Since then, they were constantly looking for new business opportunities. The satisfaction of building a profitable business was something they wanted to recreate rather than merely subsisting on a small patch of farmland. Predictably, Olof was gradually drawn into Emanuel and Erik's business dreams during their Saturday afternoon coffee gabfests, pig raising being their first venture.

"We have made some money off the pigs, but not enough," Emanuel said. "We have to find something more profitable and not as messy!"

"Messy, I'm the one doing all the skit work!" Olof cried.

"Ja, but Erik and I paid for the starter pigs."

"Let's not go through this again," Erik said. "The way I see it, if we sell or trade the pigs for coffee beans, we will all be on an equal footing."

"Ja, that makes sense," Olof said.

"Ja," Emanuel agreed, "but we sell the pigs in Umeå and then take the money to Trondheim for the coffee."

"Good idea — better than hauling squealing pigs all the way to Norge!" Erik said.

Pleased with their ingenuity, the men excitedly made their plans. Emanuel would go to Umeå and take orders for fresh pork deliveries. As it turned out, that would be the easiest part of their venture as there happened to be a shortage of fresh pork in the Umeå shops. In the meantime, Olof would write a letter to enquire about ordering a large shipment of coffee. Not knowing who the letter should be addressed to, they decided to send it to the local police station, requesting they deliver it to the proper harbor authority. This way, they figured, the deal would be sure to be legal. A month later, Olof received a response from none other than the Trondheim chief of police, Axel Paulsen, advising Olof that he passed on the message to an acquaintance at the harbor who was in the business of importing. The fortunes of the trio appeared to be looking up. The pigs were butchered and sold to the Umeå shops for a good profit, giving the partners lots of capital for their coffee venture.

The trio planned to leave in early August: a journey that would take them over the old Viking trail to Trondheim and back. First, they planned to travel to Umeå, board a freight ship to Sundsvall, where they would disembark and begin their journey over the Viking trail. They would bring two horses to pull the wagon and one saddle horse, which they would take turns riding and scouting the trail ahead. Because they had heard the trail was full of brigands waiting to pounce on unsuspecting travelers, they planned to bring their muskets, pistols, knives and swords for the journey.

Chapter 24
Gösta

"I'm just saying, the pastor's wife was flirting with me," Gösta said between swings of the ax.

"You're dreaming, Gösta," Lars said. "You're just a kid and she's a married woman. What would she want with you?" Lars was stacking the wood as Gösta split the stove length logs. Both being seventeen, and not being able to find good jobs, they would do odd jobs for area farmers, and, in this case, the pastor. Their most profitable jobs were supplying firewood to those who did not have either the time or the ability to cut their own.

"You're just jealous, Lars," Gösta said. "Wait till she brings us water. Watch how she looks at me."

They had scoured the bush around the church and parsonage for dead trees. Some were deadfalls and others were still standing. They had to be careful when chopping down these dead standing trees as large pieces would sometimes break off at the top and fall heavily straight down. The boys selected well-seasoned trees and left the rotten trees where they lay. After dragging the trees to the rear of the parsonage, they sawed them into stove length logs. Now they were splitting and stacking them in the woodshed. They had been working for the pastor for two days and were almost finished.

"How much do you think he will pay us?" Lars asked.

"I don't know. Do you think he's still sore about us moving his outhouse?"

"Ha!" Lars laughed. "That one made us legends!"

"Ja, almost worth the whipping I got." Gösta grinned.

"And the kneeling at the church!"

"Ja!" Gösta cried, "That's when she first started flirting with me, when she saw my cuk bobbing under my tunic!"

"She's three times your age, Gösta!" Lars said, "And there's many girls our age!"

"Ach, I want experienced ladies to teach me the ways of love!"

"Okay, Gösta, whatever you say."

"Here, let's trade," Gösta said, handing the ax to Lars.

Lars took the ax and moved around the stump to the pile of logs. He glanced up at the parsonage's second-floor windows just in time to see the curtains drop back in place. Someone was watching them; could have been the pastor or his wife.

"Hej, boys!" Pastor Silfversköld said as he led his horse out of the small lean-to barn. "Looks like you're almost done!"

"Ja, just this pile to go," Lars said.

"Here," he said, handing them each a riksdaler. "Make sure you finish your work before you leave!"

"Ja, sir, thank you, sir!" Lars said, pleased with the generous payment. Maybe he wasn't still angry about the outhouse prank. The pastor mounted his horse and rode out of the yard, on his way to visit some farm in the parish, making sure he arrived near dinnertime.

"You see how he was looking at my muscular chest?" Gösta said. They were both working shirtless in the heat of the day.

"Ach, you think everyone is in love with you!"

"Ja, my body is my curse. Women, and some men, will always admire it!"

They worked steadily for another half-hour and were down

to the last few logs when Camilla, the pastor's wife, came out carrying two cups. She was a pretty woman in her early fifties, far too pretty for the likes of Pastor Silfversköld with his hatchet nose and perpetual scowl. The subject was often debated after the Sunday service by men who gathered to chat, smoke and maybe sneak a taste of homebrew if someone brought some. It was a mystery to one and all, except, of course, for the pastor's wife.

"Have some cool water before you boys walk home," she said, handing the cups to them.

'Son of a gun; she IS looking at him!' Lars observed, looking over the top of his cup as he drank.

"Gösta, could I ask you to stay and help me move some furniture?"

"Ah."

"I want to surprise Jarl when he gets back late tonight."

"Who's Jarl?" Gösta asked.

"Jarl is my husband, the pastor."

"Oh, okay, we can help," Lars said.

"Oh no, I only need one of you to help."

"Ja, I will help you, ma'am," Gösta said, stammering a little. Lars noticed his face had gone red and it wasn't from the heat. He glanced down and, just as he suspected, Gösta's trousers were straining at the crotch.

"Thank you, Lars," Camilla said, extending her hand. "Say hello to your parents for me." Lars knew when he was being dismissed. He looked at Gösta, who grinned and shrugged his shoulders.

"We'll just finish up here and I will be right in, ma'am," Gösta said.

"Camilla," she corrected, placing a hand on his wrist, "call me

Camilla."

Gösta gulped, tried to answer, couldn't manage it so he just nodded.

"That woman will be the death of you, Gösta," Lars said when she shut the door behind her.

"Ja, but what a sweet death it will be!" Gösta said, grabbing Lars in a headlock and laughing. Lars tried to break the hold, but Gösta was too strong so he swung his hand up, catching Gösta between the legs. Gösta immediately let go, and fell to the ground clutching his balls.

"Ha!" cried Lars, "learned your lesson yet, Gösta?"

"Ahh, why did you do that, Lars?" Gösta hissed. "I may need these!"

"Come on. Let's quit fooling around and finish this job so I can get home," Lars said, holding his hand out to help Gösta up.

They finished stacking the split wood neatly and then cleaned up the area where they had worked.

"Seriously, Gösta, you should leave with me," Lars said. "That woman is trouble."

"I'm fine, Lars. You run along home and let a man do what a man has to do."

"Ach, I should have hit your bag harder!"

Lars watched him walk to the parsonage door. He saw Gösta raise his hand to knock, hesitate, pull back and then inhale deeply and knock. She must have called to him because he turned the knob, and glanced back at Lars with a big grin on his face before walking in and shutting the door. Lars sighed and turned to the road home. He would not see his friend again for many years.

Chapter 25
Dárjá

Lovisa had sent Dárjá to visit Tobias and had sent along a package of dried food and curtains she had weaved. But, of course, the main reason was for Dárjá to check on him and to clean his cottage. The cottage was empty upon her arrival so she asked at the neighboring farm if they knew where he was.

"Ja, he is over at Ollie's farm, helping him remove a tree root."

Following the neighbor's directions, Dárjá found Tobias and a small, wiry man in a field, sitting on large spruce logs beside a stump. Judging from the size of the logs lying around and the stump, it must have been a massive tree. The roots appeared to be as thick as a man's thigh and ran for several yards in every direction. The two men had exposed and chopped the majority of the roots and were taking a break before tying ropes around the stump for their horses to pull. Both were bare-chested with sweat streaked, dirt-covered faces and torsos.

"Hej, Toby!"

"Hej, Dárjá!" Tobias said. "This is my neighbor, Ollie Olsson."

Ollie grinned at Dárjá, a toothless grin and she would later swear his eyeballs wobbled in their sockets as he nodded his head. And not wobbling in sync with each other either! She tried not to stare at his eyes, but then found herself staring at the stump where his right forearm and hand should be. Dragging her eyes away from the amputation, she was shocked to see a number of old scars on his bare chest.

Ollie Olsson had served in the Pomeranian War as an ansättare [cannon rammer] and had lost most of his hearing. He had also lost his right arm below the elbow when he was ramming a geshwinda skott [powder and projectile in one single thin wooden cartridge] into the canon's barrel when it was fired prematurely. This sight of Ollie running in circles, screaming wildly while waving his bloody, squirting stump in the air had shocked the artillery team's young corporal so deeply that he made the idiotic decision to put Ollie out of his misery by shooting him in the chest. The pistol ball went through Ollie, knocking him backward to the ground, which only seemed to intensify the shrillness of his screams. The corporal, crazed at this point, advanced on Ollie, raised his sword over his head with both hands and was about to plunge it down into Ollie when an enemy cannonball sheared his head clean off his body. The sight of the headless corporal standing over him stopped Ollie's screams only to be replaced by hysterical laughter. When the corporal fell on top of Ollie, he put his good arm around the body and said, "Not a good time to lose your head, Corporal," followed by more hysterical laughter. Needless to say, this ended Ollie's military career and he was never quite right in the head since.

"It is good you came, Dárjá. We could use another strong horse to help us pull this stump out," Tobias said.

"Ja, I will gladly help."

"That is good!" Ollie bellowed followed by a cackle that she also found unsettling.

With three horses tied to the stump, it slowly slid out of the ground with a series of snaps and jerks. Tobias and Dárjá stopped their horses and then Tobias began yelling at Ollie to stop.

Finally, he glanced back and brought his horse to a halt.

"You should have told me it was out!" Ollie yelled.

"I tried, I was … you are right, Ollie. I should have told you," Tobias yelled back. After working all morning with Ollie, Tobias's throat was a little sore from all the yelling. Turning to Dárjá, he yelled, "So what news do you bring? Is Mamma okay?"

"I'm right in front of you, Tobias; you need not yell."

"Sorry."

"She is well; I bring food and curtains."

While they were talking, Ollie was jigging around the uprooted tree stump and flicking his arm stump up and down, cackling all the time. Dárjá gaped at him and then eased behind Tobias.

They untied their horses from the stump. Dárjá nervously glancing at Ollie, who was sitting by the tree stump stroking a large root and mumbling. "Not a good time to lose your head" and chuckling softly at his own wit.

"Adjö, Ollie!" Tobias yelled.

"Tack för den här dagen, Pehr!"

"Why did he call you Pehr?" Dárjá asked as they rode away.

"He fought with my blood father in Pommern," Tobias replied, "He always calls me Pehr; I don't mind."

"Is he touched, in the head?"

"Ja, a lot of soldiers who fought in Pommern were not the same when they came home."

"So, what news have you, brother?"

"My uncles are going to Trondheim to buy coffee."

"Really?" Dárjá replied. "All that way just for coffee?"

"Ja, they seem to have acquired a need for it ever since Mamma gave some to Manni."

"But that is such a long journey!"

"I can understand them going," Tobias said. "If I could not get my pipe tobacco, I would consider making that trip too."

"Really?"

"Ja, I can't imagine going without tobacco and I assume the same may be for my uncles and their coffee."

"Huh."

Chapter 26
The Coffee Company

One week later, Erik rode into Olof's yard and brought his horse to a stop at the water trough. The 'Coffee Company,' as they began to call themselves, agreed that Emanuel would stay behind to look after his children and to check on Olof's family now and then too. Most of their children were full-grown, but a few still lived at home. Beside Olof stood his daughter, Kajsa, who, since her abduction five years previous, begged and pleaded to go with her pappa whenever he had to travel.

The first time, Olof was going to Umeå to deliver pork and he ordered Kajsa to stay home with her mamma. Kajsa had such shockingly vivid nightmares with her pappa gone that she woke the family several times during the night with piercing primal screams that terrified her mother and her siblings. Since then, Olof's wife insisted her daughter go with Olof when the need for travel would keep him away overnight. This included trips to trade with the Sámi at their summer pasture and to Umeå to sell his pork. The trips to the summer pasture further strengthened the bond between Kajsa and Lovisa. Kajsa would stay with Lovisa in her lavvu and learn some of the skills the Sámi had taught Lovisa. They would spend hours shooting arrows at targets and, later on, hunting small game. Kajsa had become quite adept with a bow and arrow, so much so that Lovisa had the Sámi bow-maker craft her a custom-fitted bow. When Olof would look up from his trading with the Sámi and see his daughter and

Lovisa walking into the surrounding forest with their bows, he would experience a surge of pride, or maybe apprehension?

Now at fifteen, Kajsa hadn't had a nightmare in years, but she would not give up spending time with her pappa on these trips. And, truth be told, Olof couldn't imagine not taking her with him.

Erik looked at Kajsa with her garment bag in one hand and stifled his frown. He was well aware of Kajsa's nightmares from stories told and retold by his friend Olof. Kajsa watched Erik closely, holding her breath, awaiting his reaction to the prospect of her traveling with them.

"I see we have a cook traveling with us!" Erik said cheerfully. "That is good!"

Kajsa broke into a grin, dropped her bag and ran forward to embrace Erik.

Katarina came out of the cottage, wiping her hands on her apron and called, "Come and get it!"

* * * *

After their meal, Erik and Olof walked out of the cabin while Katarina and Kajsa cleaned up the dishes. The men stopped short when they saw Lovisa sitting atop a solid mountain horse in front of the cabin. Two more horses laden with furs stood behind her.

"I hear you are going to Trondheim to trade for coffee." It was more a declaration than a question.

"Ja." Olof drew out the word, not sure where this was leading.

"I will go with you. The people are out of coffee and, for some reason, it is making them irritable."

"I know!" Erik cried, "Me too!"

Olof sighed and nodded. "I am thankful for your company,

sister."

"As am I for yours, brother." She grinned.

"Lovisa!" Kajsa, who overheard the conversation, shrieked, running out of the cabin toward her. "Is it true, you are coming with us?"

"Ja, it is true."

Kajsa could not contain her excitement, dancing foot to foot beside Lovisa's horse.

"Välkommen, Lovisa, are you hungry?" Katarina asked, coming out of the cabin drying her hands on her apron.

"Ja, it has been a long ride."

"Come in then. Olof, you will leave tomorrow. Let Lovisa and her horse rest," Kerstin declared, walking back into the cabin.

As Lovisa led her horses over to the barn, Olof muttered, "I guess we leave in the morning."

"Ja, you guess right," Erik agreed. "Come, Olof, I think it may be time for a game of checkers and maybe a drop of akvavit."

Olof looked to the skies and said, "Ja, Erik, you are right. Time for you to lose another game!"

"Hah!"

Kajsa stood alone in the yard, first looking at the cabin door, then at the barn, then back again toward the cabin. Shrugging her shoulders, she walked to the cabin.

Chapter 27
Missing

"Lars!" his mother called.

It took another shake of his shoulder for Lars to wake up. His dream of Camilla, the pastor's wife, was interrupted at a most inopportune moment.

"Lars!" Louder now.

"What?" Lars muttered.

"Get up. Mårten Nilsson is he here looking for his barn," his mother said.

"Gösta?" Lars asked, coming fully awake.

"Ja," Maria affirmed.

Lars climbed out of bed, dressed and walked into the kitchen.

"Hej, Lars," Mårten said. "Gösta did not come home last night. Do you know where I might find him?"

"Last I seen him, he was helping the parson's wife move furniture."

"When was that?"

"Late afternoon. We cut and split firewood for the parsonage and she asked Gösta to stay and help her move some furniture."

"Where was the pastor?" Mårten asked.

"Off on his rounds, I guess," Lars answered. "He rode off on his horse, Cami...the parson's wife said he would be late coming home."

"Why didn't she ask for your help too?"

"I offered, but she refused, then dismissed me."

A look passed between Mårten and Laurits, which was not

lost on Maria. It was not unknown that the parson's wife had a wandering eye, although no one was aware of any infidelity.

"Tack, Lars," Mårten said, turning to leave.

"Lars will go with you, Mårten, in case Gösta's not there," Laurits said.

"Eh?"

"If Gösta's not there, Lars can take you to other places he may be."

"Ja, that is good thinking," Mårten said.

Maria wrapped some cheese and ham in a handkerchief and handed it to Lars. "Here, Lars, make sure you eat!"

Lars looked at the handkerchief, recognizing it as one of his father's, one he used to blow his nose on. His mother saw the look on his face and said, "It's clean!" Taking the package, Lars sniffed it tentatively.

"Ah, that's my favorite handkerchief!" his father said. "Many a good blow and wipe with that one!"

"Laurits!" his wife cried. "Don't tease the boy!"

Laughing, Laurits clapped his son on the shoulder and said, "Better get going, son. Mårten's not going to wait for you. Saddle the mare. Mårten will be traveling fast."

****

Lars caught up to Mårten as he was riding into the parsonage yard. Mårten walked up the stairs and across the porch floor to the door and knocked. When no answer came, he pounded on the wood with the flat of his fist. After waiting a few minutes, they walked around to the rear of the house. Mårten grabbed Lars's wrist when he noticed the rear door was ajar.

"Wait here, boy."

Mårten walked slowly to the door and peered in. Holding his hand up in a gesture meant for Lars to stay put, Mårten pushed the door fully open and edged into the house. After several minutes, Lars lost patience and entered the parsonage. Walking into the kitchen, everything looked normal, other than a few drawers left open. The sitting room was empty, so he climbed the stairs to the second story. The house was eerily quiet; even Mårten's presence yielded no noise.

Spotting Mårten standing on the second-floor landing, Lars crept up the stairs and stood behind him.

"What?" he whispered.

Mårten leaped and let out a little squeal.

"Jaysus Christ, Lars, I just about skit my trousers!" he said. "Don't do that!"

"Sorry, sir, why are you standing here?"

"Shush, listen."

They could hear someone softly sobbing from one of the rooms ahead of them.

"Hej!" Mårten called, "Is everything okay?"

They could hear hurried noises and then one of the doors opened and Camilla poked her head out into the hall. Her appearance was shocking as her face was puffy from crying and one eye was swelled and bruised purple. Her clothes were in disarray; it was obvious she had dressed in a hurry.

"My husband needs help. Please come," she said with a beckoning wave of her hand.

Mårten and Lars looked at each other and then walked to the door. They were shocked to see their pastor, Yarl Silfersköld, lying bloodied on the bed.

"What happened here?" Mårten demanded, rushing to the

pastor's side. One of Yarl's eyes was swelled shut, his nose was at a crooked angle and there was dried blood in the nostrils. He tried to speak, but it was evident his jaw was broken and all that came out was incoherent.

"Who did this, Camilla?" Mårten asked.

"It was Gösta," she said quietly, confirming what he suspected.

"Where is he?" he asked with more force than he wanted. "Sorry, Camilla; I need to find him."

She nodded and said, "I don't know. After they fought, Gösta ran out. I think he took our horse and buggy."

Mårten and Lars looked at each other, both realizing the gravity of the situation. Gösta not only defiled the pastor's wife; he beat the pastor within an inch of his life and then stole his horse. He would be hunted down and possibly shot on sight.

"I will ride to summon the doctor." Mårten sighed and walked heavily out of the room.

"Do you need help?" Lars asked Camilla. He wasn't sure how he should address her.

"Can you dump that and bring me some more water?" she asked, nodding toward a pan that held pink water and a bloody cloth.

"Ja," Lars said and carried the pan out of the room. He really wanted to run from this place but felt a responsibility to stay, at least until Mårten and the doctor arrived. *Why did I let Gösta stay?* He admonished himself, knowing there probably wasn't any way he could have deterred Gösta from going into the house and being alone with Camilla. But he felt guilty just the same.

Chapter 28
The Coffee Expedition Begins

The expedition began on a sunny Sunday morning, on August 11, 1782. Olof and Erik were busy loading the wagon while Lovisa and Kajsa packed the cooking utensils and dry goods. The men had stretched ducking material over the birch sapling bows they had bent and attached to the wagon sides. This would provide cover from the elements and keep their bedding dry.

The first misfortune of the trip occurred when Olof was struck by one of the saplings that sprung out of his hands before he could fit it into the wagon's stake bracket. The whipping sapling caught Olof on the side of his face, the force of the blow knocking him off his feet. He hit the ground on his back with an 'oof.' Erik had run around the wagon to help Olof but stopped short when a string of profanities, the likes of which he hadn't heard since the war, flowed forth from Olof's injured mouth. Olof had lost one front tooth. Both lips and left cheek were swollen and his left eye had swelled shut, the lids turning purple. The children couldn't help but laugh when he tried to drink his water the next morning at breakfast. Most of the water dribbled out of his mouth and the rest came out when Olof joined in on the laughter exposing the empty space his lost tooth once filled.

Jager, now gray with age, sat on the porch watching them and whining occasionally. He never did regain full use of his hind legs, but had become quite adept at maneuvering around in his wheelchair, that is, until old age had slowed him. Olof had sat with him that morning petting and talking to him, telling him he couldn't take him on the long journey, but he would bring him back something special from Norge. Jager's tail would wag occasionally and after a while, they just sat in companionable silence content to be in each other's company.

They rode out of the farmyard with two draft horses pulling the wagon, one Olof's and the other Erik's, two saddle horses, one Lovisa's and the other Emanuel's, and two Sámi pack horses laden with furs that Lovisa had brought to trade for coffee. Jager had tried to follow them, but Stina and Brita held him back, comforting him as he whined and howled. Eventually, they were able to lead him back to the porch where they tethered him to a post.

* * * *

Kajsa was bubbling with excitement as they began their trip; excitement the others knew would wear off before long.

"When are we going to get there?" she asked as the day progressed.

Olof winked at Erik. "I am thinking three months if we don't stop to sleep."

"What!" Kajsa cried, "Let me off. I will walk back!"

"Nej, Kajsa, you cannot do that!" Olof said, "Did you not see the forest trolls following us?"

Kajsa leaned over to look back behind the wagon from her seat on the bench.

"There are no such things as trolls, Pappa!" Kajsa said, "Stop the wagon, Lovisa. I'm getting off."

"They are teasing Kajsa. It shouldn't take more than six weeks to get there," Lovisa said, winking at Olof.

"Six weeks? We don't have enough food!"

"I hear troll meat is good if you hold your nose when you chew," Erik said.

Kajsa looked from one to the other before they started laughing. Their laughter intensified when Olof's laugh came out with a "huh huh, slurp, huh huh, slurp." Kajsa folded her arms and stared straight ahead in full pout.

"It will take about two weeks to get there, min älskling," Lovisa said. "We will save a lot of time going to Umeå and traveling by ship to Sundsvall."

"We are going on a ship!" Kajsa cried, "Yay!" her enthusiasm returning.

* * * *

After the novelty of sailing down the Swedish coastline in the Gulf of Bothnia abated somewhat, Kajsa turned to learning everything she could about sailing a cargo ship. She constantly badgered the exasperated captain and crew with questions about every detail and task no matter how small. She announced to her father one afternoon that she would become a sailor.

"Nej, Kajsa," Olof said. "Women cannot become sailors."

"Why not, Pappa?"

"Yeah, why not, brother?" Lovisa asked.

"Why, it's just the way it is," Olof stammered as both Kajsa and Lovisa crowded him until he had nowhere to back up to.

"Why?" they repeated in unison. Erik was enjoying the show, but he made sure to stay far enough back for a quick getaway in case they turned on him.

"Ahh, you should ask the captain. He knows more about

these matters than I do."

The girls stared at Olof as he shifted uncomfortably under their scrutiny and then looked at each other.

"Let's go find the captain," Lovisa said and they both turned and strode away purposefully. Olof exhaled and put a hand out to steady himself while wiping sweat from his face with his other hand. He caught sight of a grinning Erik, shook a finger at him and said, "Not a word, Erik!" Erik held up his hands in mock surrender, but he was unable to stop his grinning.

Olof and Erik followed the women at a safe distance, peeking around corners as they went. Rounding a corner of the ship's superstructure, Olof stopped Erik with a hand to his chest.

"Careful they don't see us," he whispered as Erik leaned over Olof and poked his head around the corner. Lovisa and Kajsa had the distressed captain cornered and appeared to be berating him. They could see sailors' heads poking around bales on the deck watching the encounter. Kajsa was waving her finger at the captain while Lovisa glared with hands on her hips.

"Ahh, that poor man!" Olof said, then jumped back quickly when the women turned back toward them, cracking his head hard against Erik's chin.

"Forbathke!" Erik cried, spitting blood from his bitten tongue.

"Hurry, Erik, they are coming!" Olof cried, not waiting for Erik as he ran to the other end of the superstructure. It was every man for himself as far as he was concerned.

Chapter 29
Pehr

At forty-five, Pehr was once again restless. It had been five years since his disappointing journey back to Lübeck. Although there had been much interest in the handsome businessman among the local spinsters, Pehr could not bring himself to commit to anyone. He knew he measured all women against Lovisa and so far, none had measured up or even come close. He accepted the fact that he might be alone for the rest of his days, occasionally visiting a brothel down by the docks for hurried and unsatisfying release.

It was no wonder that Pehr still lived with his friends Axel and Gunhild. Being in their company was necessary to fend off the depression that sometimes threatened to consume him. Axel and Gunhild, for their part, were more than happy to have Pehr as part of their household.

"I need a new adventure, Axel," Pehr said one evening as the two men sat smoking their pipes in the parlor.

"I know. I have noticed a restlessness about you."

"I don't want to travel, though," Pehr said. "Do you have any suggestions?"

"Hmm," Axel mused, puffing on his pipe and studying the Mora clock on the other side of the parlor. He liked the shape of it, reminding him of Gunhild when she was younger. His eyes drifted to the painting hanging beside the clock of their beloved horse, Turid. Turid gave her life protecting Pehr from a bear attack on the Viking trail eighteen years ago. The portrait was Gunhild's first and only attempt at painting and was so horribly done, it had a certain appeal.

"How about raising and selling horses?" Axel said.

"Horses?"

"Ja, Snorre Larssen, who supplies the city police with horses, is retiring and selling his business."

"Ja, remember Turid?" Gunhild asked, wiping her hands on her apron as she came in from the kitchen. "She was such a character!"

"Ja, she was," Pehr said. "It is something to consider."

"I will introduce you to him tomorrow. Now who is up for a stroll down to the tavern?" Axel asked, rubbing his hands together.

"Ja, that sounds nice," Gunhild responded. "Pehr?"

"I will go change."

Pehr had followed Axel's example of wearing a suit whenever he left the house. He had also cultivated a mustache with curled-up tips that he waxed daily and sported an expensive, custom walking stick ostensibly for his limp but likely more for appearances.

Chapter 30
Sundsvall

The Coffee Company debarked at the Sundsvall docks. The captain had his crew line up on either side of the path to the ship's gangplank and when Kajsa walked through, they stood at attention and saluted her. She was clearly surprised but quickly recovered, walking with her head held high, stopping in front of the captain who bowed low to her.

"Tack, Captain," Kajsa said with as much dignity as she could muster without giggling.

"Godspeed, Sailor Kajsa!" the captain said, straightening up and saluting.

"And to you, Captain!" Kajsa said, imitating the salute. She walked down the gangplank beaming as the sailors cheered loudly.

"That was good of them," Lovisa said to Olof as they stood watching from the dock.

"Ja," Olof said, grinning broadly at his daughter. Kajsa's eyes were moist, but she was still beaming as she came running up to them.

"Did you see that, Pappa?" Kajsa gushed.

"Ja, Kajsa, I saw it."

"I will be a sailor one of these days, Pappa!"

"Well, you may have to buy your own boat to do that, Kajsa."

"Hmm, how much is a boat?"

"I don't know. Maybe your future husband will build you

one!"

"Lars?" Kajsa replied, "He can't build anything."

"What is this?" sputtered Olof. "You are going to marry Lars Larsson?"

"Ja, whenever he gets the courage to ask."

"Humph!" Olof grunted. "Well. I guess I'm not surprised; he's always at our farm. What are his plans?"

"He will be a farmer."

"Ja?"

"Ja, he wants to be a soldier, but he will be a farmer," Kajsa said matter-of-factly.

"Does he know he will be a farmer?"

"Not yet."

Olof walked away, chuckling to himself.

* * * *

On the third day on the Viking trail, the travelers experienced their second misfortune, a torrential skyfall [rainstorm] accompanied by sixty mile an hour wind. The first sign of trouble was not noticed immediately as it came with the darkening of skies late in the afternoon. The second sign came with a complete silence, no birds signing or squirrels chattering which caused the first sense of unease among the travelers. The third sign was electricity in the air and strengthening winds that left no doubt they were in a precarious situation.

"We need to find shelter!" Erik yelled.

They had all dismounted and were trying to lead their horses down the trail into the wind. The horses were trying to turn around and were fighting the halter.

"We should go back to that cliff overhang!" Lovisa yelled

back. The wind was picking up alarmingly fast.

"That's a mile back!" Olof complained.

"It's the only shelter around here!"

Thunder cracked in the distance with such force, Olof would swear he felt it in his chest.

"Okay, let's go!"

They turned their horses and wagon around and Olof had to climb onto the wagon to operate the brake as the wind began to push it with enough force that it threatened to overtake the horses. Half a mile from their destination, the rain caught up with them and they were thoroughly drenched within seconds. Talking was out of the question at this point, everyone trying to keep from breaking into a run as the wind pushed them forward with force. Lovisa hung onto Kajsa with one hand and her horse with the other. She had tied her two pack horses to the wagon.

Kajsa turned her head to look back at her father and experienced an instance of panic as the wind snatched her breath away. The sensation was similar to when she fell off a fence rail when she was little and the breath was knocked out of her. She turned her head forward and gasped for breath. The wind whipping around her head made it difficult, so she buried her face under Lovisa's arm until, little by little, she was able to fill her lungs and breathe again. Lovisa looked at her with alarm but was mollified when Kajsa smiled and nodded her head.

They finally made it to the cliff overhang and pulled the wagon to help block the wind on one side and the horses were staked to a rope tied between two trees on the other side. Olof, Erik, Lovisa and Kajsa huddled together in the middle of the concave under the overhang, as far back as they could against the cliff wall. Olof looked up and was comforted to see the overhang was solid granite. They were out of the rain for the most part, but the wind whipped around in gusts and misted them. They all huddled with their knees up and their heads in their laps, soaked through and shivering uncontrollably. Lightning flashed and thunder boomed at such volume, it must have been very close. The horses were clearly spooked, but there was nothing they could do to calm them.

Lovisa and Kajsa screamed and they all jumped when lightning struck a tree thirty yards away. The tree exploded; pieces burst into flames momentarily, then fell across the trail. This frightened the horse to such a degree that they tore loose from the rope holding them and ran down the trail. Lovisa moved to get up but stopped when Olof put a hand on her shoulder. The storm intensified and they could hear trees crashing down nearby, causing all of them to inch back against the stone wall. Lovisa pulled Kajsa closer, protecting her against any windblown debris that may enter their precarious shelter.

The storm raged for several hours, well into the night. At some point, Kajsa dropped into a fitful sleep. She woke to birds singing, calm skies and a pleasant earthy smell. She found herself alone, clothes still damp and so she stood and pulled the cloth away from her skin. She was about to go looking for everyone when Erik came around the corner with an armload of dry wood and branches.

"This was hard to find; can you light a fire and get breakfast started, Kajsa?"

"Ja. Where is my father and Lovisa?"

"They are out trying to round up the horses," Erik said. "I'll go get some more wood. We will need more to dry these clothes."

Kajsa looked at the pile of clothes lying beside the wagon. It was obvious the others had changed into dry clothes before heading out.

"Okay, go so I can change."

After he left, she quickly changed into her only other set of clothes and immediately felt better. Once she got the fire going near the rear granite wall, the radiating heat provided another level of comfort. Her stomach growled as she set the iron trivet and kettle over the fire. *A good meal is what we need!* she said to herself.

The first one to return was Lovisa, her three horses trailing behind her. Of the group's horses, the Sámi mountain horses were the best trained and a series of whistles was all it took to bring them back.

"Olof and Erik still out?" she asked.

"Just my far. Erik is clearing trees from the trail ahead."

"That smells good, Kajsa!" Lovisa said, "I will go help look for the other horses after I eat."

"Okay, I will go look for a stream to wash these clothes."

"Nej, Kajsa, there is a stream ahead about a day's ride that I would like to stop at."

"You have been there before?"

"Ja, many years ago," Lovisa said, looking off in the distance. "This stream has special meaning to me."

Kajsa waited for her to elaborate, but Lovisa went quiet, deep in her own thoughts.

Chapter 31
Flight

Gösta abandoned the buggy near Umeå, then thought better of it and went back for it. He knew it was a risk, but he needed the money it would bring. The pastor, the son of a dog, interrupted his lovemaking with Camilla at the worst possible moment. He never heard him come into the house and then into the room. The pastor had roared and knocked Gösta off his wife and attacked him. Gösta was as furious at the pastor for being denied the pleasure that was so imminent when he was interrupted. The fight was brutal; Gösta eventually gained the upper hand and savagely beat the pastor before Camilla managed to drag him off, suffering a blow to her eye in the process. He had then forced himself on the resisting woman until he satisfied his lust.

Now Gösta was on the run. He had no doubt he would be punished severely for his transgressions. His only hope was to leave Sweden. He considered running to Norway, but that would be the obvious choice and he was sure he would be chased down and caught before he made it to the border. Going south was not an option; the distance was great and he would be caught. North was the only other option, one that would eventually take him to Finland. The Finns were no friends of the Swedes and would not assist them in their search for him. Selling the buggy in Umeå may give his escape route away, but he needed the money; he had nothing but the clothes on his back.

He had stopped at a stream to clean the blood from his face and knuckles. Seeing his reflection in the water, he was shocked to see the damage the pastor had done. He would create a diversion by letting it slip when he sold the buggy that he needed the money for passage on a southbound ship. Sighing, he steered the buggy back onto the road to Umeå without looking back. He knew he might never return home again.

Chapter 32
Memories

It was midday by the time Olof and Lovisa gathered all the horses. Erik had cleared the trail for about a mile but then crested a hill and was astonished to see a windswept stretch of the trail covered in fallen trees.

"How are we going to get through all that?" Olof asked.

"Kajsa and I can weave our way through to the other end and pull trees out of the way with the horses while you two work from this end."

"Ja, okay," Olof said. He was beginning to wonder if this venture was cursed.

The men pulled some of the trees out of the way with their horses; others they had to chop and manually carry or roll off the trail. By dusk, they met in the middle and Erik rode ahead to scout a campsite. They came up on him as he was building a fire.

"Nej, Erik," Lovisa said. "We must go another mile before stopping."

"What?" Erik cried, "What's wrong with this spot?"

"Nothing. There is a creek a mile farther and we need fresh water."

Olof knew they had enough water but learned long ago not to argue with Lovisa when she had a certain look on her face, the one she wore now. "We will keep going, Erik. Ride ahead and start a fire beside that creek."

"Ja, okay. If I don't break a leg stumbling around in the dark!"

It wouldn't get fully dark for a few hours, but no one was about to point that out as Erik stomped his fire out with more force than necessary. Lovisa appeared deep in thought for the remainder of the day's ride, so Kajsa refrained from talking. After setting up camp, Lovisa walked off on her own and sat against a tree beside the creek. This was unusual as she normally bustled around camp cooking, preparing sleeping pallets and seeing to her horses. This time, she did none of that. Kajsa saw to those tasks, sensing Lovisa needed some time alone.

It was an hour after everyone bedded down for the night when Lovisa crept into the wagon and crawled under her bedroll. Kajsa could hear the occasional sob and was at a loss as to what to do. Finally, she whispered, "Are you okay, Lovisa?"

"Ja, min älskling, I will explain tomorrow."

****

The next morning, Lovisa was quiet again, going about the daily morning tasks, cooking breakfast, cleaning utensils, packing bedding and harnessing horses.

"I will catch up with you," she said when they prepared to leave.

Olof looked at her and then said, "Okay, Lovisa, don't be too long."

"Tack, Olof."

"Can I stay with you, Lovisa?" Kajsa asked, more of a plea.

"Ja, of course, you can."

They made their way to the creek after the men left and sat down under a large tree.

"This is the last place I saw Pehr, eighteen years ago, before he was killed," she said after a few moments of silence. Kajsa waited, not wanting to interrupt.

"I cleaned his wounds while Dárjá and Toby played." She continued, "He was mauled by a bear."

Still, Kajsa kept quiet, sensing Lovisa wanted to relate the story out loud.

"The Swedish army was chasing him. He came back to see his mamma and, I suppose, me too. Of course, both his mamma and pappa were dead by then. My heart breaks every time I think of all he was put through since joining the army." She was quiet for a while so Kajsa moved closer and put her arm around her. Lovisa took a shuddering breath and Kajsa put her arms around her as she sobbed quietly.

"Okay, I am ready now," Lovisa said. Kajsa stood, then held her hand out for Lovisa. She allowed Kajsa to pull her up, feeling no shame in the fact that she needed assistance standing. "Let's catch up to the boys before they get lost."

Kajsa grinned, both at the 'boys' reference and the intimation that they would be lost without them.

Chapter 33
Stråtrövare

Olof was setting up camp in a clearing beside the trail when the stråtrövare [robbers] appeared. Erik was out foraging and Lovisa and Kajsa had not yet caught up with them. He was putting wood on the fire when they rode up, five rough-looking men on nag horses. Beside Olof was a large spruce tree where his musket leaned, out of sight. The old Viking trail was not a place to be caught weaponless, by wildlife or by desperate men.

The men spread out along the trail and stared at Olof and his surroundings, sizing him up. They had muskets and pistols across their laps, not aimed at Olof but at the ready.

"We have need of your horses." It was more of a demand than a statement.

"As do I."

The apparent leader of the band was momentarily taken aback by Olof's response, reconsidering his initial assessment of the man. He appeared unarmed and would be no match against the five of them so the leader raised his musket from his lap and started to turn it toward Olof. Olof casually reached over and, in one smooth motion, brought his musket to bear on the leader, cocking it and sliding behind cover of the tree. The leader stopped short, then laughed. Turning to his men, he gave a slight nod and they brought their muskets and pistols up and aimed toward Olof.

"I would reconsider such an action," Erik called from behind a tree several yards down the trail. The men jerked slightly and looked to their left until they spotted Erik aiming his musket at them from behind a tree. The leader sighed, still considering his options while looking around to see if there were any more hidden travelers. He was surprised to see a woman in hide clothing, aiming a bow and arrow directly at him. She had two dead rabbits tied on her belt and the bow was held steady in her hands. And, beside her, was another woman, no, a girl, who was also aiming a bow and arrow in his direction He felt an unfamiliar sensation of fear ripple through his body at the sight.

Coming to a decision, he cleared his throat and said, "Farväl, mina vänner [Farewell, my friends]," laying his musket across his lap and turning his horse.

"We are not friends and if I see any of you again, I will assume your intentions are not friendly," Olof said forcefully.

The man hesitated, then trotted off down the trail, followed by his partners. He was infuriated at being faced down, but he also recognized the danger they were in. The travelers were obviously no strangers to dangerous situations, probably veterans of the last war. But that woman! He leered at her as they passed her position on the trail, struck by her beauty and how brave she appeared to be.

* * * *

Erik walked over to Olof and they both nodded at each other. No words were necessary. Lovisa came down the trail with Kajsa practically jumping up and down as she walked, talking a mile a minute.

"That was scary. My pappa was so brave!" she gushed. "And Erik too! And you too Lovisa. Do you think they will come back?

Can I have a gun?"

She suddenly stopped, dropped her bow. Her bottom lip trembled and she ran on shaky legs into Olof's arms and stood trembling as her adrenalin subsided. Olof held her, whispering, "You are safe, min älskling. They will not be back."

Chapter 34
Trondheim, Norway

They entered Trondheim later than expected. The storm and rough condition of the trail delayed them by several days. Kajsa gawked at the hustle and bustle of the 'city,' excitedly pointing here and there and saying, 'Look at that,' as they rode through the narrow streets. Friendly residents provided directions to the constabulary; all seemed to know the chief of police when Olof mentioned Axel's name. When they arrived at the building, there was only room for their riding horses at the hitching rail so Kajsa had to stay with the wagon while the rest went inside.

Kajsa scooped some water from a nearby water trough with a cooking pot and set it in front of the wagon horses. She was stroking one of the horse's neck as it drank when she saw a man walking in her direction on the boardwalk. He was well-dressed and had a slight limp. There was something very familiar about him as he came to a stop between her and the building's large window.

"Oh, my, those are fine horses!" he said.

Kajsa nodded, not sure how to respond to this handsome man.

"And this one too," indicating Lovisa's mare. "Where are they from?" he asked.

"They are my auntie's horses, mountain horses," Kajsa said with some pride.

"Do you know if they are for sale?"

"Nej, they are not."

"Svenska?"

"Ja."

"Me too!" he said with enthusiasm. "Once, anyway."

He turned and looked into the window's green-tinged wavy glass and saw Axel talking with a small group of people.

"I guess Axel is busy; I will have to come back later." Turning back to Kajsa, he bowed slightly and said, "Adjö, min kära [Goodbye, my dear]!"

Kajsa blushed furiously and stood speechless as she watched him walk away, one hand on her chest between her small breasts.

"Are you ill, daughter?" Olof asked as he came out of the building.

Again, the blush came and she stammered, "Ja, I mean, nej, ahh what?"

"There is room in our stables in the back if you need to put your horses up," Axel said. They all stood on the boardwalk, Lovisa watching Kajsa with a slight smile.

"Ja, that would be good!" Olof said, "Tack!"

"You can stay above my favorite tavern — clean rooms and good food," Axel added, "Tell the owner I sent you."

"Tack, sir."

"Call me Axel. After you put your horses away, I will walk with you down to the docks and introduce you to the importer I wrote about."

"What a nice man," Lovisa said after he walked back into the building. She then steered Kajsa away from the rest. "You met a boy?"

"Nej!" Kajsa cried.

Lovisa looked at her until Kajsa said, "An older man, very

handsome and rich!"

"How much older?" Lovisa asked.

Kajsa shrugged and said, "Like Pappa."

"Oh, Kajsa, he is too old for you."

"What, nej!" she cried. "He just admired your horses and then he called me 'dear!"

They giggled and put their foreheads together.

"What are you two up to back there?" Olof called.

"Nothing, Pappa." And more giggles.

Chapter 35
The Paulsens

"I stopped by the constabulary this afternoon but saw you were busy with some strangers," Pehr said. He and Axel had moved to the parlor for their nightly smoke after a rather fine meal of herring and new potatoes.

"Ja, travelers from Sverige looking to buy coffee beans."

"Coffee beans?"

"Ja, coffee. Seems to be a shortage in Sverige."

"Huh," Pehr said, "they did have some fine horses."

"Why were you stopping by my work?" Axel asked.

"I wanted your opinion on a business matter."

"Ja?"

"Ja, I told my workers I was considering selling the store and venturing into the horse business."

"Ja? That is wonderful, Pehr!" Axel said, "And I can give you advice on the business of horses."

"But that is not the advice I was seeking."

"Oh?"

"Ja, my workers want to purchase the shop; lock, stock and barrel."

"Well, it is good you have buyers already, but are you sure you want to sell?"

"Ja, I am sure. The problem is, they don't have near enough to pay what the shop is worth."

"Oh, I see your dilemma," Axel said, looking at the Mora

clock as he was prone to do when pondering a problem.

Gunhild came in with her coffee and sat in her customary chair. "You have made a small fortune over the years from that shop, most of it sitting in the bank. Why not give the shop to your workers for a small percentage of the profits for as long as the shop is in business?"

"Gunhild, that is a good idea!" Pehr said, "Why did I not think of that?"

"Because my wife looks out for everyone, including your workers," Axel said, patting her hand.

"Now, that calls for a proper drink. Anyone interested in going down to the tavern?" Gunhild asked.

"Ja, I promised to meet the coffee buyers there this evening," Axel said. "Pehr?"

"Tack, but I think I will go tell my workers about the offer," Pehr said, anticipating their reactions. "But could you ask if they would consider selling me one of their fine mountain horses for breeding?"

"Ja, I can do that."

****

Olof, Erik, Lovisa and Kajsa sat at a table, having finished their evening meal. Kajsa was still excited about being in a tavern. "Wait until I tell Lars," she gushed, "that I was sitting in a tavern before he could!"

"Well, you won't be sitting here much longer, Kajsa," Olof said. "This is not a place for a young lady!"

"Aww. Are we leaving?"

"Come, Kajsa, let's go see to the horses before it gets dark," Lovisa said.

"Ja, okay," she grumbled but dutifully followed Lovisa out the door. Axel and Gunhild entered a minute later.

"Hej Axel," Olof called, "over here!"

Gunhild looked over at their usual table, sighed and followed her husband over to the stranger's table.

"Hej, Olof, Erik, this is my wife, Gunhild."

Both men surprised her by standing respectfully, Erik pulling her chair out for her.

"Did you make your deal for your coffee?" Axel asked.

"Ja, we made a good purchase. Lovisa needs to find a buyer for her furs before she can buy her coffee."

"Furs?" Gunhild asked.

"Ja, she is from a Sámi tribe and she is my sister."

"Are you Sámi?" Axel asked, clearly doubting him.

"Nej, I mean, she is like my sister; she lived at our farm."

"Ah, and you are still close?" Gunhild asked.

"Ja, we are."

"Just like us and Pehr," Gunhild said.

Olof choked on his ale, leaning over and coughing. Erik reached over and slapped his back.

"Sorry, I had a brother named Pehr, dead these twenty years," Olof said after he recovered.

"Has it been twenty years?" Erik asked. "I think maybe eighteen..."

"You could be right, Erik."

"It is a common name," Axel said. "Our Pehr, he is going into the horse raising business and he wanted me to ask if you would consider selling him one of your mountain horses for breeding."

"Oh, those are Sámi horses," Olof said. "I doubt they would sell."

"Okay, how are you liking the rooms here?"

"They are clean, like you said."

"That is good!" Axel said, "Now, who wants another drink?"

Chapter 36
A Nice Lunch

"I suppose Lars and I will get married next year when I am sixteen," Kajsa answered. They woke early and were reluctant to rise, both content to remain under the covers. She and Lovisa shared a bed while Olof and Erik were in the next room.

"I don't think Olof and Erik will be up for a while; they came in quite late, singing and knocking things over," Lovisa said. "Wait, did you say, Lars?"

"Ja."

"What about that old man who made you blush?"

"What old man?"

"The one who called you dear."

"Ah, he was a handsome man," Kajsa mused. "I wonder if he will teach me how to perform my wifely duties."

"What!" Lovisa shrieked and then they both broke into laughter. They laughed harder when they heard pounding on the wall followed by a muffled 'quiet!'

"He did remind me of somebody, but I can't think of who," Kajsa said after a while.

"Who?"

"The man on the boardwalk — he reminds me of someone. It has been bothering me that I can't figure it out."

"Ah well, it's not important," Lovisa said. "We should get up. Do you want to come with me to sell my furs?"

"Ja!"

"Okay, let's go eat. The boys won't be getting up anytime soon."

****

They began their search for a buyer at the docks, then working their way into the business district without any luck. They went back to the tavern to get ready to go to the Paulsens. Gunhild had insisted they all come for the midday meal at their home. After washing up in their room, Lovisa knocked on the boys' door and heard a grunt. She tried the handle and found it unlocked.

"Förbaske!" she cried, covering her nose, "it stinks in here!" Olof and Erik were still lying in bed, looking like they were dragged behind a horse and smelling worse.

"Get up, ya lazy arses!" she cried, kicking Olof's bed.

He responded with a loud and wet sounding fart.

"Fek!" she cried. "Your daughter needs money to buy clothes and I need some until I can sell my furs."

Olof waved toward his trousers lying across a chair. She went over, rooted through the pockets and took what she estimated they would need. She then walked over to the only window in the room and pulled the curtains apart, causing groans from both men who covered their heads under blankets. She opened the window and then left the room, slamming the door behind her, satisfied when she heard a muffled groan.

They followed directions to the Paulsens' given to them by the hotel manager, who also asked how long Olof and Erik were planning to stay. He seemed disappointed when Lovisa said at least another night. It was a short walk and Gunhild excitedly ushered them to the dining table, talking nonstop and fawning over Kajsa. Pehr had left a few minutes before they arrived, late for a meeting with his workers and his solicitor, preparing to transfer ownership of the shoe store.

"Oh, how I wish I could have had a daughter just like you!"

"How come you don't?" Kajsa asked.

"It wasn't in the stars, little one."

"The stars?"

"Ja, the stars, where all the fates of man reside," Gunhild said. "I am a bit physic, so I am. Would you allow me to read your future?"

Kajsa had her back to Axel so she couldn't see his warning.

"Ja, I would like that!" she said.

"And you, Lovisa?" Gunhild asked, turning to look at her.

"We may not have too much time, Gunhild," Lovisa said. "After our meal, I need to find a buyer for my furs and Kajsa needs to buy clothes." She had seen the alarm in Axel's eyes and rightly guessed she should avoid Gunhild's offer.

"Ah, I think I have a buyer for you!" Gunhild cried. "Mathias Nilsen, the tailor! He who makes fur cloaks and wraps."

"That is good, Gunhild, tack!"

"I will take you there after my reading of Kajsa's future!"

"Uh, what if I don't like what you see in my future?" Kajsa asked.

"That is the risk you must take, but it may also be good."

Kajsa noticed Lovisa shaking her head slightly, so she said, "Maybe I shouldn't…"

"Are you sure, Kajsa? I feel a strong aura around you," Gunhild asked.

"Ja." Kajsa sighed.

"Okay, that's settled. Now let's eat!" Axel said, rubbing his hands together. "It is regrettable that Olof and Erik are not feeling well!"

Gunhild gave him a knowing glance and then began placing plates and bowls on the table.

Lovisa and Kajsa gaped at all the food. Spread before them were potato dumplings, jellied fish, pickled herring, a lamb dish and, for dessert, crumb cake. All the food was delicious, Gunhild beaming as they ate heartily, complimenting her after tasting each new dish, that is, except for the pickled herring, which was common in Sweden. Axel excused himself as soon as the meal was finished, having pressing work waiting for him at the constabulary.

"Are you sure you would not like a reading?" Gunhild asked, pouring coffee into their cups. Kajsa sniffed the drink, not having tried it before. She shook her head and then tentatively sipped and made a face that caused Lovisa to smile.

"It takes a little getting used to, min älskling."

Wanting to be a grown-up, drinking a grown-up drink, Kajsa took another sip, made a sour face and pushed the cup away.

"Come, let's go sell your furs!" Gunhild declared, hiding her disappointment at not being able to read Kajsa's future.

They walked three abreast down the cobbled street, Gunhild nodding at houses along the way, commenting on each woman of the house's shortcomings whether it be lack of cooking skills, cleaning habits or frequency of yelling at their husbands. Walking past one house, she confided that the woman who lived there seemed to have a lot of men sneaking in through the rear door whenever her husband was away at sea. Lovisa wasn't sure if she should believe her new friend, never hearing of such goings-on before now.

"There is Nilsen's shop. I will introduce you to Mathias, then let you bargain with him," Gunhild said.

Kajsa was tugging on Lovisa's sleeve as they neared the shop.

"What?" Lovisa asked.

"Could I go across the street and look at the shoes?" Kajsa whispered. Lovisa nodded and told her to wait there for her. Kajsa nodded and made her way across the street, stopping halfway to let a wagon pass. The driver tipped his hat to her as he passed. I could get used to this place, she thought.

Entering the shoe store to the sound of the small bell above the door, she breathed deeply, enjoying the aromas of leather and sweet pipe tobacco. She was surprised to see the man from the previous day, the one who had called her 'dear,' come through the curtained doorway at the rear of the shop.

"Hej, I remember you!" Pehr said, "Välkommen!"

"Tack."

"How can I help you?"

"I need a pair of shoes."

"You are in luck, dear. This happens to be a shoe store!"

Kajsa flushed at the term of endearment so much so that she didn't notice Pehr's attempt at humor.

"Are these shoes for church and school or to wear around the farm?" Pehr took in her threadbare clothing and rightly assumed she lived on a farm.

"Ah, both?" Kajsa stammered. She hadn't thought about that.

"It is your lucky day!" Pehr said. "I am having a 'going out of business sale' and the shoes are two pairs for the price of one!" He made this up on the spot, feeling generous in his last couple of days as the owner of the shop. He also felt a strange kinship with this little girl and felt pleasure in providing her with what was obviously much-needed shoes.

"Oh, that is good! How much will my shoes cost?"

"Five skilling." A very low price for his quality of shoes, but an amount he was confident she could afford.

"Tack," she said, not aware that the price was extremely low, but knew she had more than enough to pay that amount. Lovisa had given her shopping money earlier and remembered seeing several coins with skilling marked on them and in several different denominations.

"Sit here. I will take some measurements," Pehr said, indicating a chair that had a stool in front of it. Kajsa sat and allowed Pehr to take her foot and remove her shoe. Pehr inspected the shoe. Seeing how crude and poorly made it was, he set it aside and took her bare foot in his hands. If he noticed her sharp intake of breath, he gave no indication.

"I will build your shoe to support your heel," he said, turning her foot and running his hand along the bottom of her arch. "You see how your foot is not flat?"

All she could do was nod. Her face and neck were hot and there were butterflies in her stomach. There was also a strange sensation between her legs that alarmed her but also thrilled her.

"Your foot is not flat so your shoes should not be flat either," he continued. "How high would you like the uppers?"

"The what?" she croaked.

"How high do you want your shoes to rise?" he asked. "I would suggest to here." He slid his hand up her lower calf, stopping halfway up.

"Is that okay?"

All she could was nod, the blush engulfing her neck and face, even her scalp above and behind her ears. He brought out a cloth tape and started taking measurements. At this point, Kajsa was quite enjoying the attention her foot was getting.

"Okay, I have everything I need. They will be ready tomorrow morning," Pehr said.

"What about the other foot? I will need both shoes."

"Hah!" He laughed, then said, "Oh, you are not joking. Is your right foot different from your left?"

"Ja."

"Okay," he said, then removed her right shoe and began measuring. Kajsa had to clamp her lips together lest a sigh escape her.

"Well, there is no difference between your feet," Pehr said.

"Ja, there is. This one is my right foot and that one is my left foot."

"Hah, you are right!" Pehr laughed and then slid Kajsa's shoes back on, holding each calf with one hand and the shoe with the other. Kajsa left the shop in a daze, smiling dreamily and had to put her hand on a hitching rail to steady herself as she let out a 'whew!'

"Kajsa, are you okay?" Lovisa asked, coming across the street. "You look flushed."

"Ja, just a little warm."

"Are you sure, dear?" Gunhild asked.

Kajsa stiffened at Gunhild's use of 'dear,' feeling that it should only be used by the shoemaker. She didn't even know his name! "Ja, I am okay." Turning to Lovisa, she asked, "Did you sell your furs?"

"He is interested," Lovisa said. "We need to go load the furs and take them to him."

"Okay."

"Then I will take my leave," Gunhild said. "Please come for dinner this evening and bring the men too."

"Dinner?"

"The evening meal."

"Oh, ja, we will come, tack."

"Adjø!"

"Adjö!"

"Lovisa?" Kajsa asked after they walked a few yards.

"Ja?"

"What does it mean when you get a tingling between your legs?"

"What!" Lovisa cried, "When did that happen?"

"When the shoemaker was measuring my feet for shoes."

Lovisa grabbed her arm and giggled. "Was he handsome?"

"Ja, he was…. Lovisa?"

"Ja?"

"The shoemaker was the man who called me 'dear' yesterday."

"Nej!" Lovisa teased. "The old man?"

"He's not old!"

"Oh, Kajsa, we need to have a talk this evening!"

Lovisa sold the Sámi furs for less than expected, but the amount was enough to purchase as much coffee as her horses could carry, with a little traveling money left over. They arranged to pick up the coffee the following day. After putting the horses back in the stables, they walked downtown to do some clothes shopping. Kajsa was having the time of her life.

Chapter 37
A Nice Dinner

"Where are you going, Pehr?" Gunhild asked.

"I am making two pairs of shoes for one of your guests, the young girl."

"Kajsa?"

"Is that her name?" Pehr said, picking at a piece of ham.

"Can you wait a little while to meet them?"

"Nej, I will be working into the wee hours as it is."

"Okay." She sighed. "Maybe you will meet them before they leave tomorrow."

"Ja, Kajsa will need to come and collect her shoes. I can meet them then. Adjö!" he said, walking out the door.

Pehr walked down the side of the street. There was no boardwalk here. In the distance, he could just make out the tavern where four people had exited and were walking his way. After many years of laboring over shoes, his long-range vision had suffered. Should he wait for them and introduce himself? Nej, it would be less awkward to meet tomorrow. He turned at the corner and continued on toward his shop.

"Is that the old man that makes you tingle?" Lovisa whispered to Kajsa.

"Lovisa!" Kajsa cried, pushing her.

"What is that?" Olof asked.

"Nothing, Pappa," Kajsa said.

Olof wasn't convinced especially with Lovisa's snickering.

"Is that the famous Pehr, the Paulsen's boarder?" Erik asked, nodding toward Pehr just before he turned off the road they were on.

"Did you say Pehr?" Lovisa asked.

"Ja, it's a common name. This one looks like a proper gentleman." Olof said.

"Our Pehr could have been a proper gentleman, if he had the chance."

"Ja, I suppose he could have been," Olof said quietly.

They were still a few blocks away from where Pehr turned off. At that moment, Olof had a shock of recognition but just as quickly dismissed it. It was not the first time that had happened. Once, several years after the Pomeranian War, he was walking down a street in Umeå and was convinced he saw his late brother Jakob walking ahead of him. He had run up to the man and had to apologize to him after grabbing his arm and stepping in front of him, realizing his mistake.

"I'm sorry you missed your old man, Kajsa," Lovisa whispered, grinning mischievously.

"Ach!" Kajsa growled, scowling at her.

They enjoyed a good meal and Lovisa declined on the group's behalf of the offer to have a 'few' drinks down at the tavern. She did not want a repeat of the other night for Olof and Erik. They had a long trip home and she did not want to have to fight with them to get moving in the morning. Instead, they went for a pleasant walk along the shores of the Trondheim fjord.

Chapter 38
Departure

Early the next morning, Lovisa and Erik led the Sámi pack horses down to the docks to load the coffee beans that she had purchased. Meanwhile, Olof and Kajsa walked to the shoemaker's shop to pick up her new shoes.

"How much are these shoes?" Olof asked.

"Five skillings."

"Hmph." Olof was skeptical about the quality of the shoes if they were so cheaply priced. "Well, don't get your hopes up; they may not be what you expect."

Kajsa was wearing a bright dress she had bought the day before. Her worn-out, old shoes stood out in contrast. She was excited to see her new shoes.

"Come on, Pappa!" she said, tugging on his hand.

"Slow down; we will get there."

Kajsa was about to reach for the shop's door when it swung open and Axel exited.

"Kajsa! Pehr says your shoes are all finished," he said, then turning to Olof, "May I have a word with you?"

"Ja, of course," Olof answered. "Go ahead, Kajsa. I will be right in."

"Okay, Pappa," Kajsa said, rushing into the shop and slamming the door in her haste.

"Välkommen, Kajsa!" Pehr called from behind the counter, "Your shoes are ready. Have a seat and let's check the fit."

Kajsa hurried over to the seat she sat in last time. Pehr smiled, proud that his craftsmanship could cause so much excitement. He looked out the green-tinted, wavy glass windows and saw Axel and another man on the boardwalk.

"Is that your father?" he asked.

"Ja."

"I would very much like to meet him, but let's try these shoes on first."

He sat on his stool, put one hand on her calf and slid her left shoe off and then slid the new shoe on. Kajsa looked in awe at the shiny black leather shoe with a brass buckle on the front. She had never seen anything as beautiful as this shoe. And it fit perfectly! Pehr repeated the process with the other shoe and then asked her to walk around the room.

"These are perfect!" she cried, "and so comfortable!"

"That is good! Now let's try these," Pehr said, unwrapping a paper package and removed high-top, lace-up shoes with a built-up heel. These were also made with shiny black leather. Kajsa gaped in disbelief at these shoes. They were beyond anything she had ever seen before.

"I'm sorry, Kajsa. Are they not what you wanted?" Pehr asked, alarmed at the tears in her eyes.

"They are the most beautiful things I have ever seen," Kajsa said, wiping her eyes. "Are they for me."

"Ja, they are for you."

She sat back in her chair and let him remove her new shoes and put the high-top shoes on her. She was so enamored with her shoes; she didn't notice his touch this time.

"Now walk around," Pehr said.

As Kajsa walked around the shop, Pehr looked out the

window, noticing Axel and Kajsa's father were still standing out there, talking and laughing.

"They are perfect!" Kajsa cried. "Can I wear them now?"

"Of course, they are yours."

"Tack!" she said, handing over a five-skilling coin.

"Tack, Kajsa," he said, accepting the coin and then slipping it into one of her old shoes when she wasn't looking. He wrapped the other new pair in paper and tied the package with twine. "Would you like your old shoes wrapped too?"

"Ja, I can wear them in the barn and pens."

"It has been a pleasure serving you, min älskling!" Pehr said, bowing slightly. "Have a safe journey home."

Kajsa blushed at the intimacy and stammered, "Tack." She went to the door, looking back before exiting and returned his smile.

"Wow!" Olof said, taking in her shoes, "those might be the nicest shoes I have ever seen!" He was suspicious of the quality of the shoes and the cost Kajsa told him. He was sure she paid a lot more than a mere five skillings. He would have to talk to her when they were alone.

"Ja, Pehr is a master when it comes to shoes," Axel said.

Olof looked through the glass into the shoe shop, but it appeared empty. This Pehr must have gone into the back room, probably his workshop. He had a sense of knowing this mysterious shoemaker, but the reason remained hidden in his brain.

"Safe travels, my friend!" Axel said, holding out his hand.

"Tack," Olof responded, shaking the proffered hand, "and we are grateful for your assistance and hospitality."

"So long, Kajsa."

"Adjö, sir," she replied as he walked away.

"Here come Erik and Lovisa," Olof said, spotting them as they steered the wagon down the street toward them. He could see Axel waving at them until they stopped the wagon beside him. "Come, let's go save them; Axel will talk their ears off if we let him!"

"I thought you wanted to meet Pehr?" Kajsa said.

"Ja, maybe next time. We are wasting the day standing around chatting."

"Kajsa!" Lovisa cried when they walked up to the wagon. "Those shoes are beautiful!"

"Tack," Kajsa said, turning this way and that, showing off her shoes.

"Do we have time for me to get a pair of shoes?" she said, half in jest to the obviously impatient Olof.

"Nej! Let's go!"

"He called me min älskling!" Kajsa whispered to Lovisa after she climbed up beside her on the wagon bench. Lovisa snapped her head toward her quickly, shocked that a stranger would use such an intimate phrase with a young girl. She looked toward the shoe shop and could see the outline of someone standing at the glass looking out at them. She had a strange sense of recognition and thought, I know this man.

"Let's go!" Olof bellowed, having mounted Lovisa's horse. She sighed and flicked the reins, looking back once more at the shop.

Chapter 39
Pehr

Pehr watched the group down the street and a feeling of recognition passed through him. Did I meet these people when I was a young man in Sverige? He wished he could have met them before they left, but something always seemed to come up. I think I will go outside and introduce myself before they leave, he decided, grabbing his frock coat.

"Pehr?" Kristian called from the cutting room.

"Ja?"

"Could you come back here? I have a problem with this pattern."

"Ja," Pehr sighed, returning his coat to the rack. Maybe next time, he thought, disappointed he could not meet the strangers and talk to them about the mountain horses.

****

The following evening, Pehr and Axel sat in the parlor smoking theirs pipes in companionable silence.

"I never did get a chance to meet your visitors, the coffee buyers," Pehr said. "Just the girl, Kajsa."

"Oh?" Axel said, studying his pipe. The tobacco had gone out. Time to give it a good cleaning, he thought.

"Ja, I was hoping to see if I could convince them to allow me to breed some of my mares with one of their studs. I think the result would be a sturdier version of what I have."

"So, you are buying Snorre's business?"

"Ja, we made the deal and just have to sign the documents at the solicitors."

"That is great news, Pehr!" Axel cried, getting to his feet, grasping Pehr's hand and pumping it.

"Hilda!" he hollered. "Come, we must go down to the tavern and celebrate Pehr's new venture!"

"Ja? Congratulations, Pehr!" she called from the kitchen. Coming into the parlor, she said, "I suppose a celebratory drink is in order."

****

Pehr and Gunhild settled into their usual chairs in the tavern as Axel went to get their drinks. He insisted on buying the drinks, the first round anyway.

"A toast!" Axel cried as he set their drinks down and raised his, "to our newest horse breeder, Pehr Olofsson!"

The tavern's patrons, mostly regulars acquainted with Pehr, all cheered enthusiastically. So much so that Axel yelled, "A round of drinks on me!" Then discreetly checked his money pouch. The cheering reached a crescendo followed by men coming over and shaking Pehr's hand. Axel was a little put out that they didn't acknowledge him for the drinks. Gunhild reached over and patted his hand with a smile. She always knew his moods and thoughts, and how to make him feel better despite them.

"Will you be making shiny leather shoes for those horses, Pehr?" yelled an inebriated man. Everyone laughed uproariously, those near the man clapping him on the back, which evoked a toothless grin. "With shiny brass buckles?" he added, but the moment had passed and his remark was met with only a few chuckles.

They stayed longer than usual, due to the occasion, they told themselves.

"This will be the last one!" Gunhild admonished as Pehr placed the latest round of drinks on the table.

"Ja," Axel slurred and winked at Pehr, "the last one."

"Are you changing anything, Pehr?" Victor Bøhler, the iceman, said, on his way to the door, "in the way Snorre has operated his business?"

"Not so much. I would like to breed more stamina in the horses though."

"How are you going to do that?" he asked, clearly interested.

"There are mountain horses from Sweden, which I would like to breed my mares with."

"You mean Lovisa's horses?" Gunhild asked.

Pehr sprayed his ale across the table, narrowly missing Axel.

"What did you say?" he asked after coughing several times.

"Lovisa; her horses," she replied.

"Well, not really her horses. The Sámi's horses," Axel corrected.

"Lovisa Öhn?" Pehr demanded.

"Ja, that sounds familiar. Did she not say that, Axel?"

"Ja, I think so."

"Tell me!" he demanded, grabbing Axel's forearm, squeezing hard. "Who was with her?"

Axel grasped Pehr's wrist and pulled until Pehr loosened his grip. "You are not behaving like a gentleman, Pehr," he said sternly.

"Sorry, Axel, but I need to know. Who was she with?"

"Her brothers, Olof and Erik," Gunhild interjected. "Although, they're not really her brothers. It's all very confusing how they are all related."

They looked at Pehr with concern as he sat back in his chair, ashen-faced.

"Are you okay, Pehr?" Axel asked.

"Ja, Lovisa Öhn is my, was my fiancé before I went to war," Pehr said quietly. "Olof is my brother and Erik, my friend."

Axel and Gunhild looked at him in shock, Axel asking, "Why didn't you say anything when they were here?"

"I didn't know it was them!" he cried, downing the rest of his ale in one gulp. "I must go to her, before they cross the border."

"You can't leave now," Gunhild said. "It's dark and you are drunk!"

"Hilda is right, Pehr." Axel said, "You get some sleep and I will have a horse and supplies ready for you before first light."

Pehr hesitated, then seeing the wisdom in the plan, nodded.

"You are right, Axel, tack. But I doubt I will be able to sleep!"

* * * *

Pehr did manage to sleep, albeit a fitful sleep, waking several times through the night from dreams he could not remember. Each time he jerked awake; it would take long minutes before he would drop off again. By morning, he was not as well-rested as usual but still functional. Axel was true to his word; two impressive saddled horses stood in their rear yard and two bulging haversacks sat by the back door.

"I put your pistol in there too, Pehr," Axel said. "As you know, the trail is a dangerous place."

Several years previous, Pehr had accepted a French double

barrel pistol in exchange for a pair of riding boots from a retired French military officer. Pehr and Axel would often go shooting in the countryside, to keep Axel's marksmanship up and because Pehr enjoyed the shooting. The pistol was meant for close quarters, so Pehr took to setting targets at 20 feet. It took many hours of practice before he became quite skilled with the weapon, at least at close range.

"Tack, Axel."

"And I will be going with you."

"What?" Pehr said. "I can manage on my own."

"Nej, Pehr, Axel will go with you!" Gunhild said from her place by the stove. "After what happened to you last time, I will not allow you to travel that road alone!" She said this with hands on her hips and the look on her face told Pehr not to argue. Turning to Axel, Pehr said, "I am grateful for your company, Axel."

Gunhild, as expected, had loaded a canvass sack with food enough to last for weeks and was now serving up a large breakfast.

Pehr cleaned his plate and, when Gunhild tried to serve him more, he said, "It is time, Hilda."

"Ja." She sighed.

They walked out to the horses, Gunhild hugging both men and telling each to be careful. Axel turned to Pehr and said, "Let's go get her, son!"

Chapter 40
The Long Road Home

"You should put your new shoes away, Kajsa," Lovisa said. "They will get ruined out here."

They were sitting beside each other on the wagon's bench, Kajsa with her feet on the toe board, admiring her shiny shoes. She had changed out of her new dress and wrapped it in paper.

"Ja, okay." She sighed, climbing over the bench into the wagon bed, being careful not to scuff her shoes on the way. She found the package containing her old shoes and unwrapped it. After carefully taking off her new shoes and lovingly wrapping them in the paper, she slipped her old shoes on, feeling something in the toe of one. She took the shoe off and shook it until something fell out. It was a five-skilling coin! Is this the same coin I paid to the shoemaker? she thought to herself. Why would he do that? Were the shoes meant as a gift? If so, it was a very nice gift, almost as nice as the hunting bow Lovisa had given her a few years ago. Should she tell Lovisa about it or her father? Maybe not; they would not understand and her father would want the money back. No, it was best to keep this a secret, her and the shoemaker's secret, feeling a thrill thinking about it.

It was late afternoon on their second day of travel home when they stopped for a midday meal. Olof had insisted upon a hot meal instead of eating dried meat when the others wanted to keep going. Lovisa suspected it was all a ruse so he could make his coffee. Lovisa had argued to no avail that they should take advantage of the daylight as the sun would set sooner once they were in the mountains. Now the sun was low in the sky and darkness was near.

Erik had scouted several miles ahead and then changed horses to scout their rear, in case they were followed by anyone with bad intentions.

"Did you hear that, Lovisa?" Kajsa asked after hearing the distinct sound of a grouse beating its wings.

"Nej, what did you hear?" Lovisa had heard but pretended she hadn't.

"A grouse, 50 yards that way," she said.

Lovisa tried not to smile but could not help it; the pride she felt for Kajsa was too great.

"That is good, Kajsa!" Lovisa said. "Do you need help?"

"Nej, I will go get him," Kajsa said matter-of-factly, picking up her bow and quiver and striding confidently through the brush, quiet as a fox.

Olof had watched the exchange with interest.

"She has confidence because of you," he stated.

"Nej, she always had confidence. I just showed her how to use it."

"Tack, Lovisa, for everything."

"It was my pleasure, Olof."

It was not long before Kajsa came out of the bush, carrying a grouse.

"That will make a good soup, Kajsa!" Olof exclaimed.

Kajsa beamed as she carried the bird over to the fire.

*****

The next evening, the Coffee Company was setting up camp

after a good day's travel. Olof once again wanted to stop at midday to make coffee, but this time, he was outvoted three to one. They had been climbing all day and stopped when they crested one of the Scandinavian mountain's foothills. Kajsa, as usual, was tasked with starting and maintaining the fire. She took the tin with flint and steel Dánel had given her out of her shoulder pack and set about the making of fire. It spoke to her character, and possibly the times, the contents of her shoulder pack did. Inside were sinew snares, two knives, arrowheads, a carved wooden cup and her five-skilling coin.

Lovisa and Olof had erected the tents, one, an army-style tent and the other, a Sámi lavvu. They were now sitting by the fire watching Kajsa cook the evening meal. Erik had returned from scouting the trail ahead and would scout the rear after his supper. They had earlier passed through a spruce forest, collecting half a dozen squirrels, courtesy of Kajsa's archery skills. Together with chives foraged by Lovisa, the aroma coming from the cooking pot hanging above the fire evoked rumbles from their stomachs. They were chatting about the day's travel when Lovisa quieted the others with a raised hand.

"Shush," Lovisa whispered.

Before they could react, the five stråtrövare they had encountered on their previous trip over the mountains emerged from the bushes on either side of the camp and surrounded them. Faced with muskets and pistols aimed directly at them in close quarters, Olof and company raised their hands.

"Victor, Herman, collect their weapons," the leader, Knut, ordered.

After the two men gathered the weapons, Knut said, "Put them in the wagon. We will take that too."

"What are we going to do with a wagon?" Victor asked.

"It's loaded with something; we will sell it all in Trondheim. Ove, Petter, tie them up."

They tied Olof and Erik back to back and the same with Lovisa and Kajsa.

"Stop that!" Lovisa yelled when Ove cupped her breasts after tying the women.

"Leave them be. We will have plenty of time for that after we eat," Knut ordered, picking a squirrel out of the pot and sitting on a stump to eat. "Mmmm, that's good!" he said as he started gnawing on the carcass.

The others each grabbed a squirrel and raced to finish theirs in order to get one of the remaining two squirrels in the pot. Knut grabbed one and tossed the other in the general direction of three of his men, laughing uproariously as they all dove for it like dogs.

"Is that coffee I smell?" Victor asked. "It is!" he answered himself by sniffing the pot sitting by the fire. Olof looked at them in disgust as they poured his precious coffee into cups and slurped loudly. "Ah, that's good!" Victor said, grinning at Olof.

After they finished eating and drinking Olof's coffee, Ove went to his horse and came back with a jug. He poured out generous helpings into outstretched cups. To their captive's dismay, the captors raised their cups and said, "Skål," leaving no doubt that they were drinking alcohol.

"Do you have a plan, Olof?" Erik whispered.

"Nej," sighed Olof, "I fear what they have planned for the women."

"I don't know if I can bear to see or hear that happen, Olof."

"Nor I," Olof said. He had been trying to twist his wrist so he could work at the knots without much success. "See if you can work the knots loose, Erik."

"Okay."

They were watching the men drinking, gauging their level of drunkenness. There was a sense of urgency, to get loose before they went for the women.

****

"Are you okay, Kajsa?" Lovisa asked.

"Ja, should I soil myself so they will leave me alone?"

"Nej, we will not degrade ourselves; I don't think that would stop them anyway," Lovisa said, "but we will fight with all our strength!"

Chapter 41
The Chase

Pehr and Axel were riding fast when they crested a hill and caught sight of Olof's group across a large valley. They stopped to watch them, to see if they could recognize them from this distance. All Pehr could tell was that it was one man on horseback and a wagon. He couldn't tell who or how many people were on the wagon. They watched until the wagon disappeared over the hill and were about to chase after them when they spotted the others.

Five men on horseback emerged from the bush alongside the trail not far from the hill and rode slowly up the rise. They were being careful and stealthy about their movements, which alarmed Pehr. People only move like that when they are tracking someone or something. Pehr dismounted and took his pistol out of his pack and loaded it. Axel followed suit and then both men leaned low over their saddles and kicked their horses into a gallop.

They crossed the valley at full gallop and slowed when they approached the crest of the hill. This was not the first time Pehr came across ill-intentioned people on this trail. Seeing no sign of anyone, they dismounted, tied their horses to scrub brush and climbed the last few yards to the top of the hill. Crawling the last few feet, they peeked over the top and down the trail. In the distance, they could see Olof's group setting up camp on top of the next hill. He could also see three of the men following them hiding behind willows halfway between their position and Olof's camp. The other two men were working their way up a draw paralleling the trail. The draw petered out near the crest so the men would have to bush wack the remaining way to the camp, if that was their intention.

It was getting late in the day and Pehr voiced his concern to Axel. "I fear they may attack the camp after dark."

"Ja, that is my concern, also," Axel said. "Look! They're charging the campsite!"

From their position, a mile or so away, they could see the action taking place. It looked like the bandits caught Olof's group by surprise, which puzzled Pehr. Thankfully, no shots were fired, so everyone was okay, for the time being.

"Looks like they are tying them up," Axel said.

"Ja, let's get close and plan our next move."

"If we keep to the left and ride in single file, we may be able to get close to their position undetected."

"Okay, let's go!"

Chapter 42
Captivity

The captors were becoming belligerent. They had finished their alcohol and had thrown everything out of the wagon until they found Olof's crock of akvavit. Kajsa was infuriated when her dress and shoes were thrown on the ground. She fought back tears as she watched one of the men step on her dress and grind his heels, all the while looking at her with a sneer.

Kajsa was surprised when the thought entered her mind, He would be sorry if Jäkel were here! Why would she think that? Her father and Erik were tied up and could do nothing to stop these men. But she still should have thought of Manni, or Toby, not Jäkel. And Jäkel was dead. Strange why she wished he was here to save her. After all, he had abducted her and held her captive in a cave. She looked at Lovisa and was surprised to see her staring at her with a look of, what exactly?

"What?"

"Nothing, min älskling," Lovisa responded. "I just wish I could protect you."

"It is enough that you are here with me. It is frightening when I am captive all by myself."

"Oh!" Lovisa gasped, "I am sorry my husband did that to you."

"It is okay; he did not hurt me and it is not your fault he took me."

"Okay, Kajsa, this is what I want you to do." Lovisa

whispered, "When they come for us, kick them as hard as you can between their legs!"

"It will hurt those little sacks they have?"

"Yes, very much!"

"That reminds me, what are those things for?" Kajsa asked. "The little sacks."

"You don't know?"

"Nej, I saw Lars's a few years ago when he was swimming with no clothes on. Me and Stina and Maria saw him and his friends."

"Ah, your mother never told you?"

"Nej."

"Hmm, how do I say it?" Lovisa pondered. "Inside those sacks are seeds."

"Seeds?"

"Ja, for growing babies. They plant those seeds inside a woman and a baby grows."

"Nej!" Kajsa breathed. "You mean like planting potatoes?"

"Ja, I suppose."

"Huh. And the hill around the potatoes is like how a belly gets big?"

"Nej, Kajsa, it is the baby growing."

"Wait!" Kajsa said, "Will I have one of their babies if they force themselves on me?"

"Maybe."

"Then I will fight to the death when they come for me!" She spat out the words with conviction. Lovisa nodded, pleased with Kajsa's resolve. The light was fading as she listened to their captor's voices rising in argument.

"The older one is mine; the rest of you can have the young

one!" Knut said.

"Why can't I have the older one too?" Victor demanded.

"Because she is mine and I don't want you ruining her with your filth!"

With a roar, Victor leaped up and dove across the fire at Knut, knocking him over. They rolled to the middle of the road, punching and grunting as the others jumped up and cheered them on. Olof and the other captives watched with interest as this happened, each hoping they two fighters would kill each other. Kajsa was the first to hear the horses. "Someone's coming," she said loud enough for Olof and Erik to hear.

They all strained to hear over the fighting and shouting and could hear the hoofbeats getting louder fast. Out of the darkness, two horses with riders leaning low over their saddles charged into the men, knocking the three spectators down and trampling over the fighters. Two shots rang out and then the riders disappeared down the road.

"Push against me, Erik," Olof said. "Let's try to stand."

Erik braced his back against Olof's and pushed upwards and backward with his legs.

"Not so hard, Erik!" Olof's legs were not as strong as Erik's.

In the glow of the fire, the captives watched as Knut and Ove slowly stood. The other three lay unmoving in the road. Olof and Erik made it to their feet and Olof said, "Let's go!" They both let out their regiment yells and tried running sideways toward the fray. Their feet tangled up after a few steps into their valiant charge, both falling into the dirt with a pair of "oofs." Despite the situation, Lovisa snorted at the sight.

Before Knut and Ove could react, the two horsemen came charging through again. They dove on opposite sides of the road as the horses charged through. The riders leaped off their saddles, tackling the two men. From where he lay, Olof recognized Axel as he fought with Ove. He couldn't see what was happening on the other side, just two indistinct shapes rolling on the ground.

Axel made short work of Ove, clubbing him with his pistol and then securing his wrists behind his back with a pair of iron handcuffs. From his knees, Axel looked across the road at the other two combatants, as did Olof's group. All they could see were dark shapes, one on top who raised a knife and plunged it down. The struggle stopped as the person on top caught his breath. He turned and looked back toward Axel and then stood and began walking toward him. Axel looked around for a weapon, other than his empty pistol. Seeing nothing, he stood and faced the approaching figure.

"Are you okay, Axel?" Pehr asked.

"Ja, are you?" Axel's relief evident in his voice.

"Ja." They stood before each other and put their hands on each other's shoulders. Nodded and turned toward the captives.

"Löva!" Pehr said, rushing toward her, "are you okay?"

"Pehr?"

Pehr knelt and untied the binds, Kajsa staring at him with huge eyes. Lovisa turned and threw her arms around Pehr. Kajsa went over to where Axel was untying Olof and Erik.

"I am glad to see you, Axel!" Olof said, "And I am grateful to you for bringing me my brother!"

Kajsa stood watching Pehr and Lovisa hugging each other tightly, Lovisa with shuddering sobs. She asked her father, "What is happening?"

"My brother Pehr, your uncle, he who was thought dead

these eighteen years," Olof said.

"Pehr, Lovisa's Pehr?" Kajsa asked.

"Ja, and Tobias's father."

Pehr whispered in Lovisa's ear, "my brother," and tried to disengage the embrace. Lovisa squeezed harder, then let go and nodded. Pehr turned and walked to Olof, nodding at Erik before embracing his brother.

"Good to have you back, Pehr!" Olof said.

"Good to be back!"

"Erik, good to see you again!"

"And you, Pehr!" Erik said, shaking his hand. "You have more lives than a cat, my friend!"

"And I know this pretty lady," Pehr asked, turning to Kajsa, who blushed furiously, "but are we family?"

"Ja, I am your niece. This is my pappa," Kajsa said, indicating Olof.

"Nej, you can't be!" Pehr exclaimed. "You are much too pretty to be Olof's daughter!"

Kajsa was grinning broadly at the flattery, still beet red and one foot kicked backward as she giggled, covering her mouth shyly. Lovisa was amused as she watched the interaction.

"Erik," Axel said, "could you give me a hand?"

"Ja."

"We need to cover these bodies until I can transport them back to Trondheim."

"Ja," Erik sighed. "I do have some experience in these matters."

Chapter 43
New Beginnings

Early the next morning, Lovisa joined Axel by the fire while everyone else slept. Axel's prisoner sat against a tree several yards away, chin on chest and apparently asleep. The others had talked into the early morning hours before exhaustion forced them to bed.

"God morgen, Lovisa."

"God morgon, Axel."

"I am surprised you are up so early."

"Despite all the excitement of our rescue, and I thank you for your part in that, and with being reunited with Pehr, I had the best sleep in many years!" Lovisa said.

"Pehr is my friend; I would fight beside him anytime," Axel said. "It is good to see him happy again."

"He has not been happy?"

"It is hard to tell with him," Axel sighed. "Pehr never talks about it, but he has a depression."

"What is this depression?"

"He has been through so much misfortune and loss; it sometimes overwhelms him and he feels sad for a long time. Gunhild and I would notice when the depression comes and we would spend a lot of time with him and try to keep his spirits up."

"That is sad. Do you think he will get better?"

"I don't know, Lovisa. It is a mysterious affliction."

They sat quietly for several minutes, both within their own thoughts while staring into the fire.

"I will do my best to make him happy, Axel," Lovisa said, breaking the silence.

"Pardon my candor, but you live far away, in Sweden, and Pehr cannot travel there."

"I am moving to Trondheim in the spring to marry Pehr," Lovisa said. "We discussed it last night and Pehr proposed marriage to me!"

"That is good to hear, Lovisa!" Axel cried, "And my wife will be happy to hear this too!"

"It is the first time anyone proposed to me."

"Really, but you were engaged to Pehr and you were married to that Sámi man?"

"Ja, and both times I had to propose!" Lovisa laughed.

Not far from where Lovisa and Axel were sitting, Kajsa lay listening to their conversation. Several emotions ran through her, concern for Pehr and his history of depression, happiness for Lovisa, sadness that she would be living far away from her, and jealousy? Why would she feel jealous? She would be marrying Lars soon enough. Maybe because Lovisa and Pehr were so obviously in love with each other while Kajsa and Lars were, what exactly? Would they ever have the same love as Lovisa and Pehr? Rising, she was determined to show happiness for her friend, whom she always thought of as her aunt, and her newfound uncle.

"God morgon, Kajsa," Lovisa said.

"I heard you talking," Kajsa said, leaning down to hug her. "I am happy for you, Lovisa!"

"Tack, Kajsa."

"Will I ever see you again, after you move to Norge?"

"Of course. Pehr and I discussed hauling coffee to Brattby for Manni and Olof to sell, along with some horses."

"Ja, can Pehr go there?"

"I think it will be safe if we travel to the people's summer pasture and then along the Umeå River to Manni's farm. After eighteen years and with his mustache and a hat, no one will recognize him."

"The people?"

"The Sámi."

"But how will I see you?"

"We will come visit you and Lars, and your twelve little ones!"

"Ach!" Kajsa cried, much to the amusement of Axel.

They parted ways at noon, Olof and Erik on horseback, Lovisa and Kajsa on the wagon. Pehr and Axel stood in the middle of the road, waving every time someone looked back at them.

"It did my heart good to see family again, Axel."

"Ja, but you know, Pehr," Axel said. "Hilda and I are your family too."

"Ja, you are. And soon, Lovisa will be a part of our family."

"It is good, Pehr. Now let's go home."

"Ja, home."

The Radermans
Albert Sandberg
Paperback ISBN: 9781590955208
eBook ISBN: 9781590955215

The story of the Raderman family is an epic tale of four brother's journey from their farm in northern Sweden to war torn Prussia in 1756.

The youngest brother, Pehr, leaves behind his childhood sweetheart and fiancé, Lovisa Öhn, vowing to return to her after the war.

The Pomeranian war rages for seven years and their love for one another will be tested both on the battlefield and at home.

While Pehr and his brothers endure the horrific conditions in war torn Prussia, Lovisa forges her own legacy as a respected mid-wife for both Swedish and Sámi women.

Unforgettable characters and events throughout the story.

The Radermans Series Book 1

CPSIA information can be obtained
at www.ICGtesting.com
Printed in the USA
LVHW032300090320
649432LV00005B/486